HERGÉ
★
THE ADVENTURES OF
TINTIN
★
TINTIN
IN
AMERICA

LITTLE, BROWN AND COMPANY
New York   Boston

Artwork © 1945 by Casterman, Paris and Tournai.
Library of Congress Catalogue Card Number Afor 1107
© renewed 1973 by Casterman
Library of Congress Catalogue Card Number R 558598
Translation Text © 1978 by Methuen & Co. Ltd. London
American Edition © 1979 by Little, Brown and Company (Inc.), N. Y.

Little, Brown and Company

Hachette Book Group
237 Park Avenue, New York, NY 10017
Visit our website at www.lb-kids.com

Little, Brown and Company is a division of Hachette Book Group, Inc.
The Little, Brown name and logo are trademarks of Hachette Book Group, Inc.

ISBN: 978-0-316-35852-1

Library of Congress catalog card no. 79-64865

30 29 28 27

Published pursuant to agreement with Casterman, Paris
Not for sale in the British Commonwealth

Printed in China

TINTIN IN AMERICA

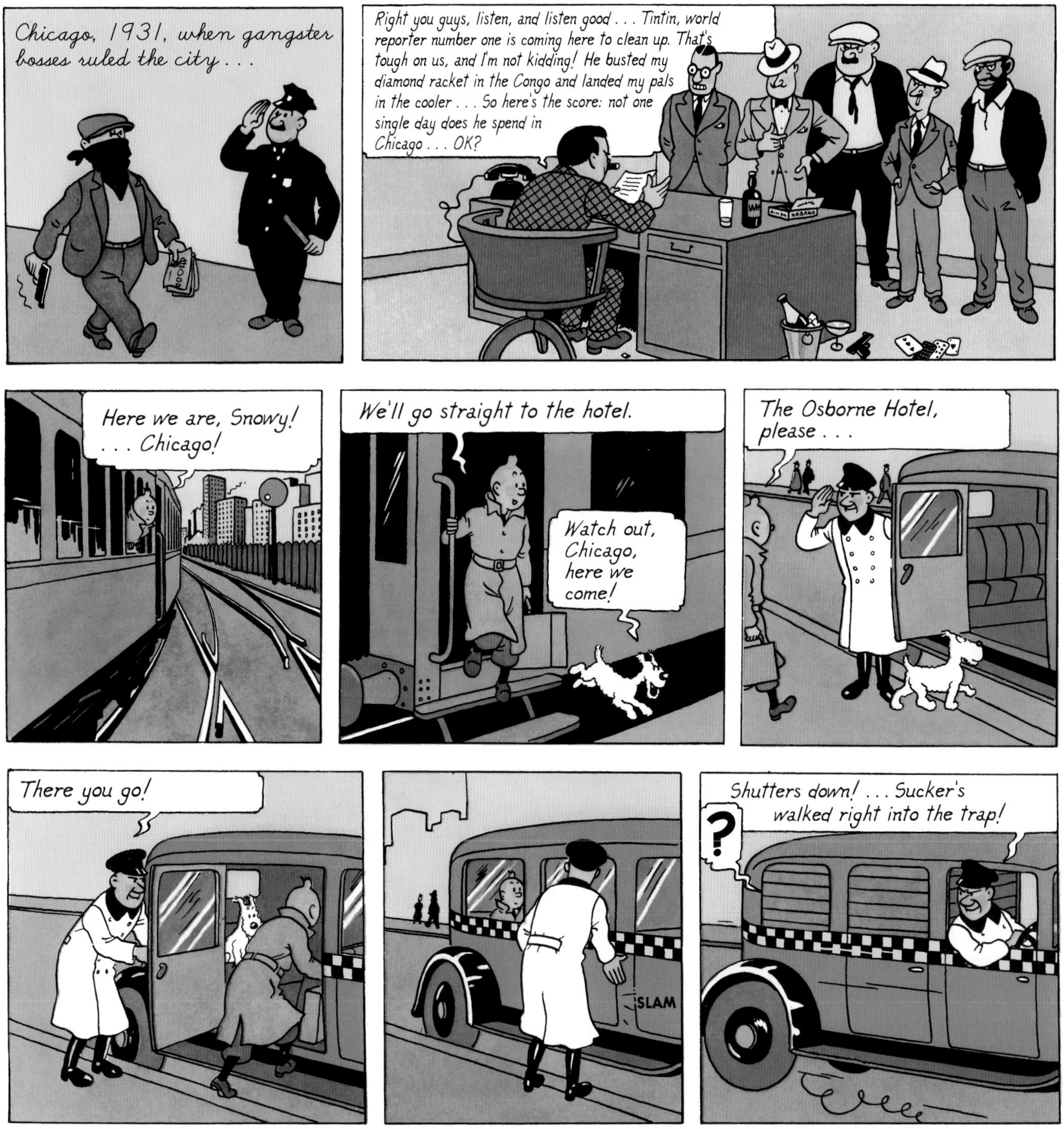
Chicago, 1931, when gangster bosses ruled the city . . .
Right you guys, listen, and listen good . . . Tintin, world reporter number one is coming here to clean up. That's tough on us, and I'm not kidding! He busted my diamond racket in the Congo and landed my pals in the cooler . . . So here's the score: not one single day does he spend in Chicago . . . OK?
Here we are, Snowy! . . . Chicago!
We'll go straight to the hotel.
Watch out, Chicago, here we come!
The Osborne Hotel, please . . .
There you go!
SLAM
Shutters down! . . . Sucker's walked right into the trap!
?

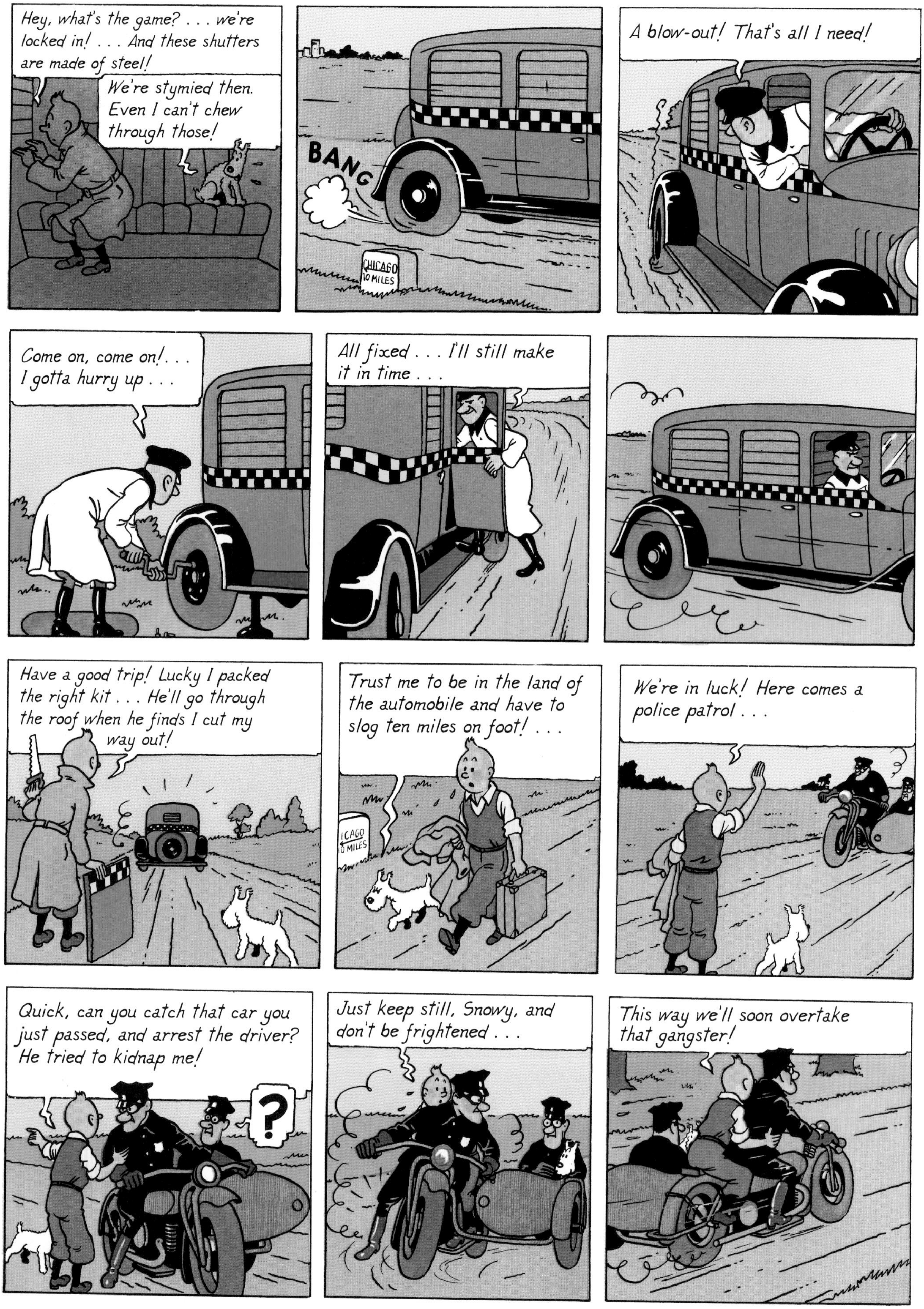
Hey, what's the game? . . . we're locked in! . . . And these shutters are made of steel!
We're stymied then. Even I can't chew through those!
BANG
CHICAGO 10 MILES
A blow-out! That's all I need!
Come on, come on!. . . I gotta hurry up . . .
All fixed . . . I'll still make it in time . . .
Have a good trip! Lucky I packed the right kit . . . He'll go through the roof when he finds I cut my way out!
Trust me to be in the land of the automobile and have to slog ten miles on foot! . . .
We're in luck! Here comes a police patrol . . .
Quick, can you catch that car you just passed, and arrest the driver? He tried to kidnap me!
?
Just keep still, Snowy, and don't be frightened . . .
This way we'll soon overtake that gangster!

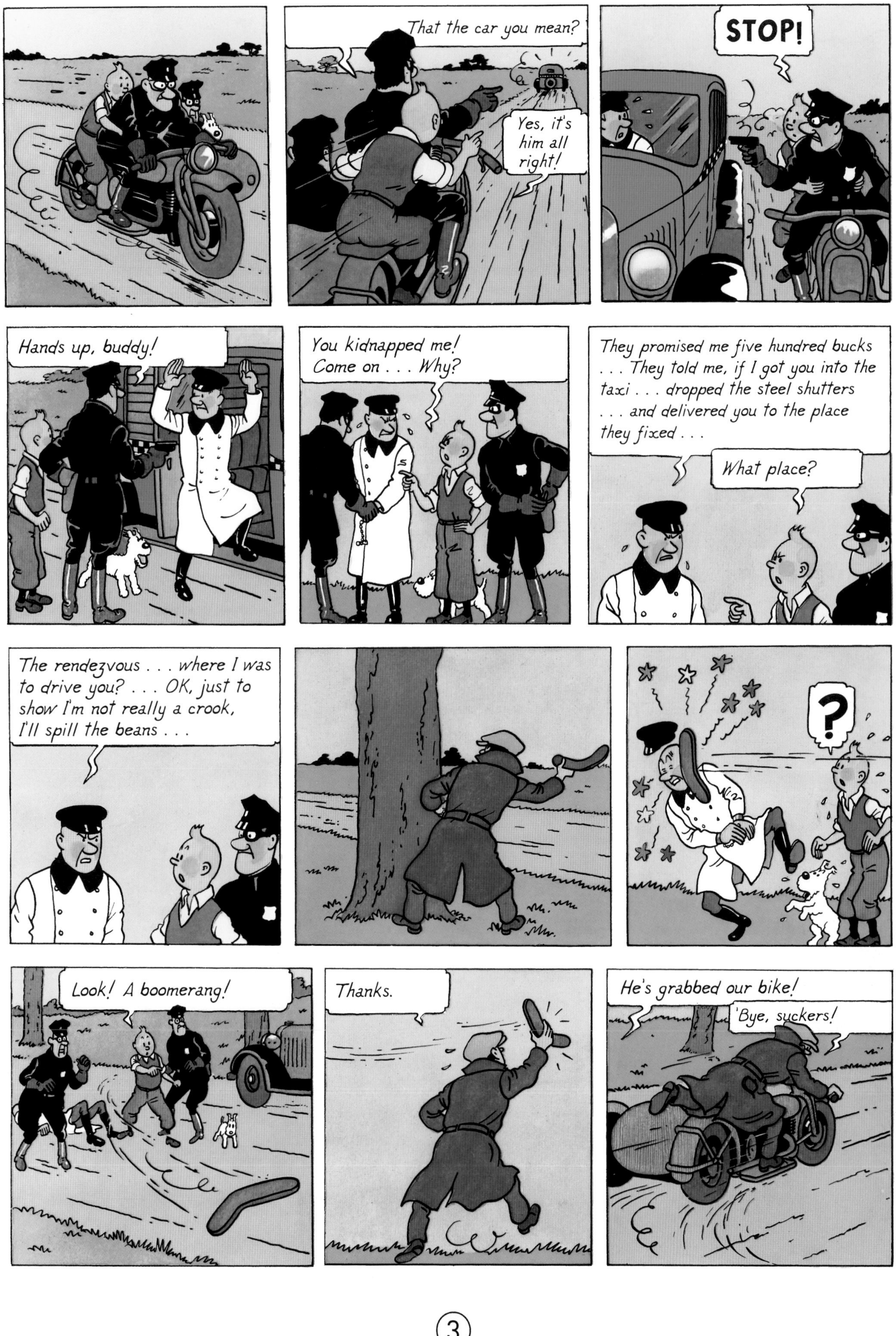
That the car you mean?
Yes, it's him all right!
STOP!
Hands up, buddy!
You kidnapped me! Come on . . . Why?
They promised me five hundred bucks . . . They told me, if I got you into the taxi . . . dropped the steel shutters . . . and delivered you to the place they fixed . . .
What place?
The rendezvous . . . where I was to drive you? . . . OK, just to show I'm not really a crook, I'll spill the beans . . .
?
Look! A boomerang!
Thanks.
He's grabbed our bike!
'Bye, suckers!

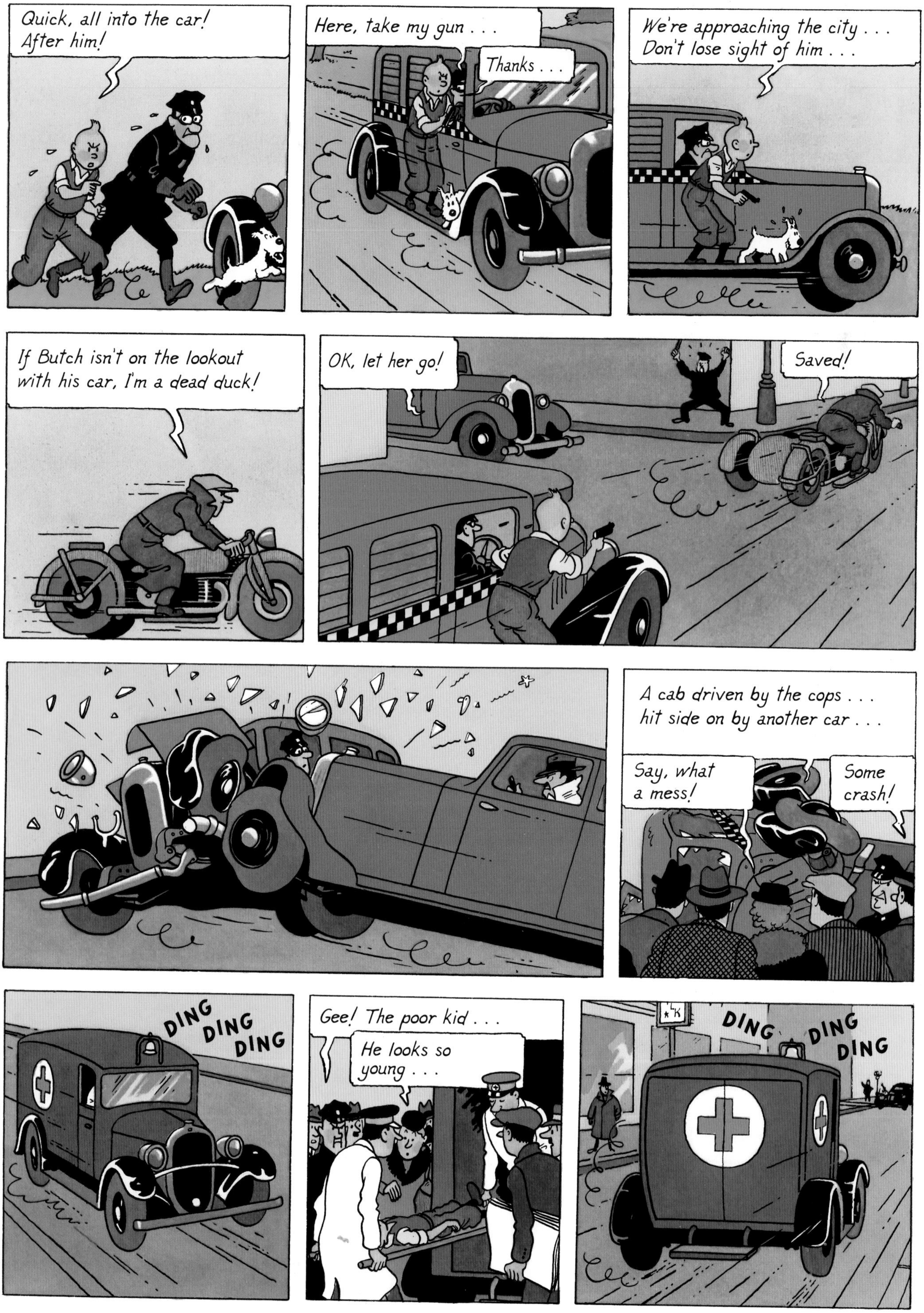

Quick, all into the car! After him!
Here, take my gun . . .
Thanks . . .
We're approaching the city . . . Don't lose sight of him . . .
If Butch isn't on the lookout with his car, I'm a dead duck!
OK, let her go!
Saved!
A cab driven by the cops . . . hit side on by another car . . .
Say, what a mess!
Some crash!
DING DING DING
Gee! The poor kid . . .
He looks so young . . .
DING DING DING

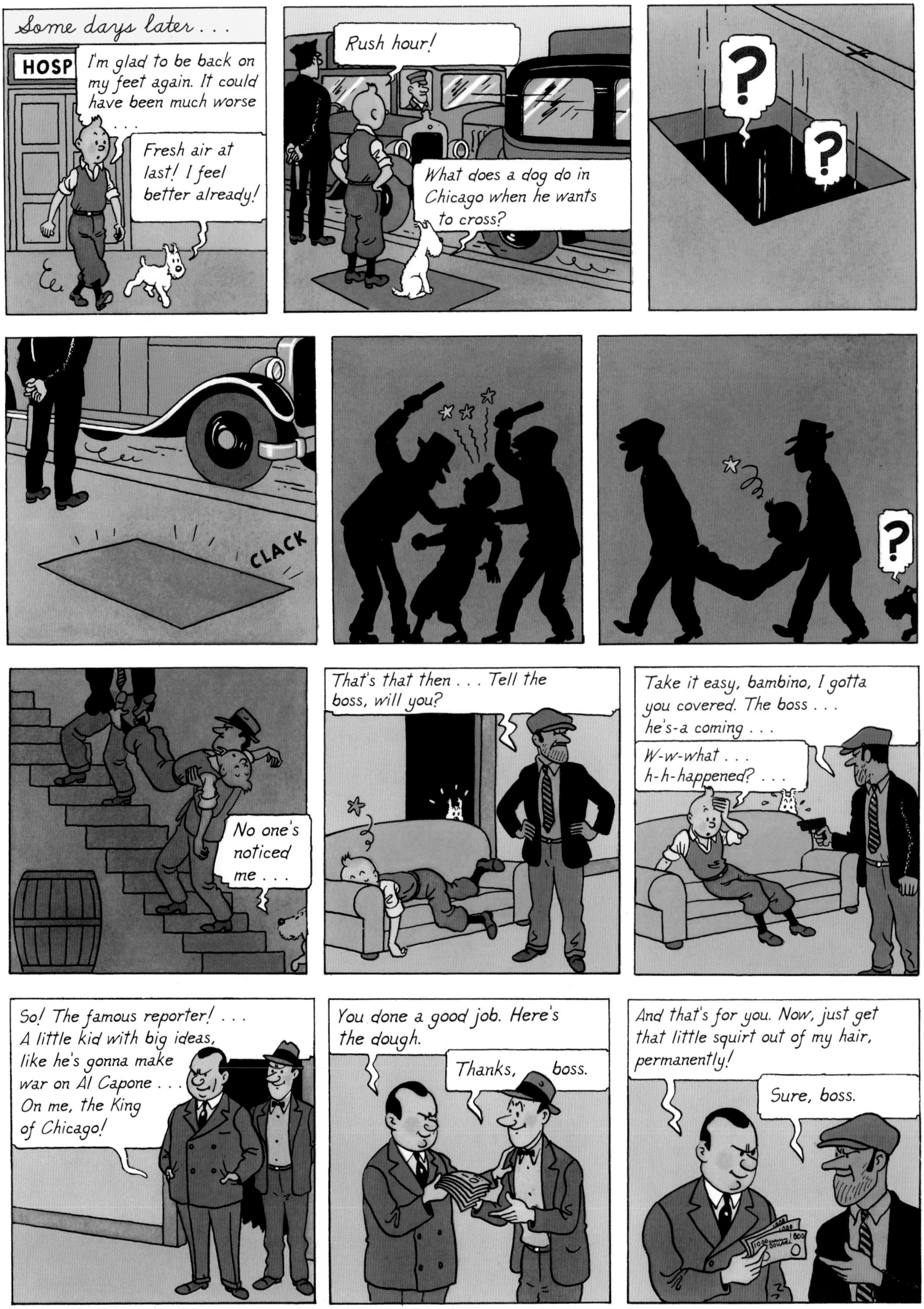
Some days later . . .
HOSP
I'm glad to be back on my feet again. It could have been much worse . . .
Fresh air at last! I feel better already!
Rush hour!
What does a dog do in Chicago when he wants to cross?
?
?
CLACK
?
No one's noticed me . . .
That's that then . . . Tell the boss, will you?
Take it easy, bambino, I gotta you covered. The boss . . . he's-a coming . . .
W-w-what . . . h-h-happened? . . .
So! The famous reporter! . . . A little kid with big ideas, like he's gonna make war on Al Capone . . . On me, the King of Chicago!
You done a good job. Here's the dough.
Thanks, boss.
And that's for you. Now, just get that little squirt out of my hair, permanently!
Sure, boss.

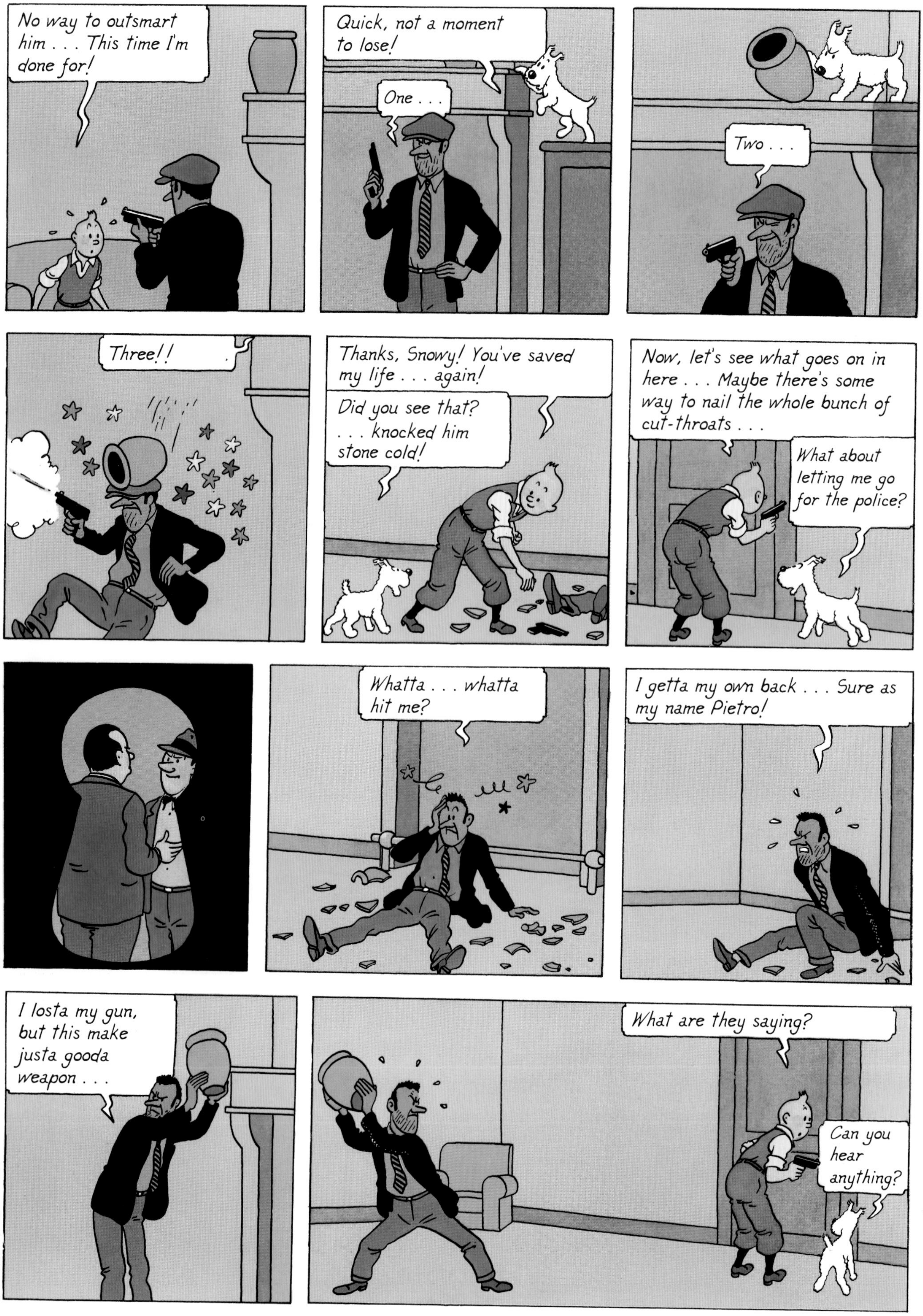
No way to outsmart him . . . This time I'm done for!
Quick, not a moment to lose!
One . . .
Two . . .
Three!!
Thanks, Snowy! You've saved my life . . . again!
Did you see that? . . . knocked him stone cold!
Now, let's see what goes on in here . . . Maybe there's some way to nail the whole bunch of cut-throats . . .
What about letting me go for the police?
Whatta . . . whatta hit me?
I getta my own back . . . Sure as my name Pietro!
I losta my gun, but this make justa gooda weapon . . .
What are they saying?
Can you hear anything?

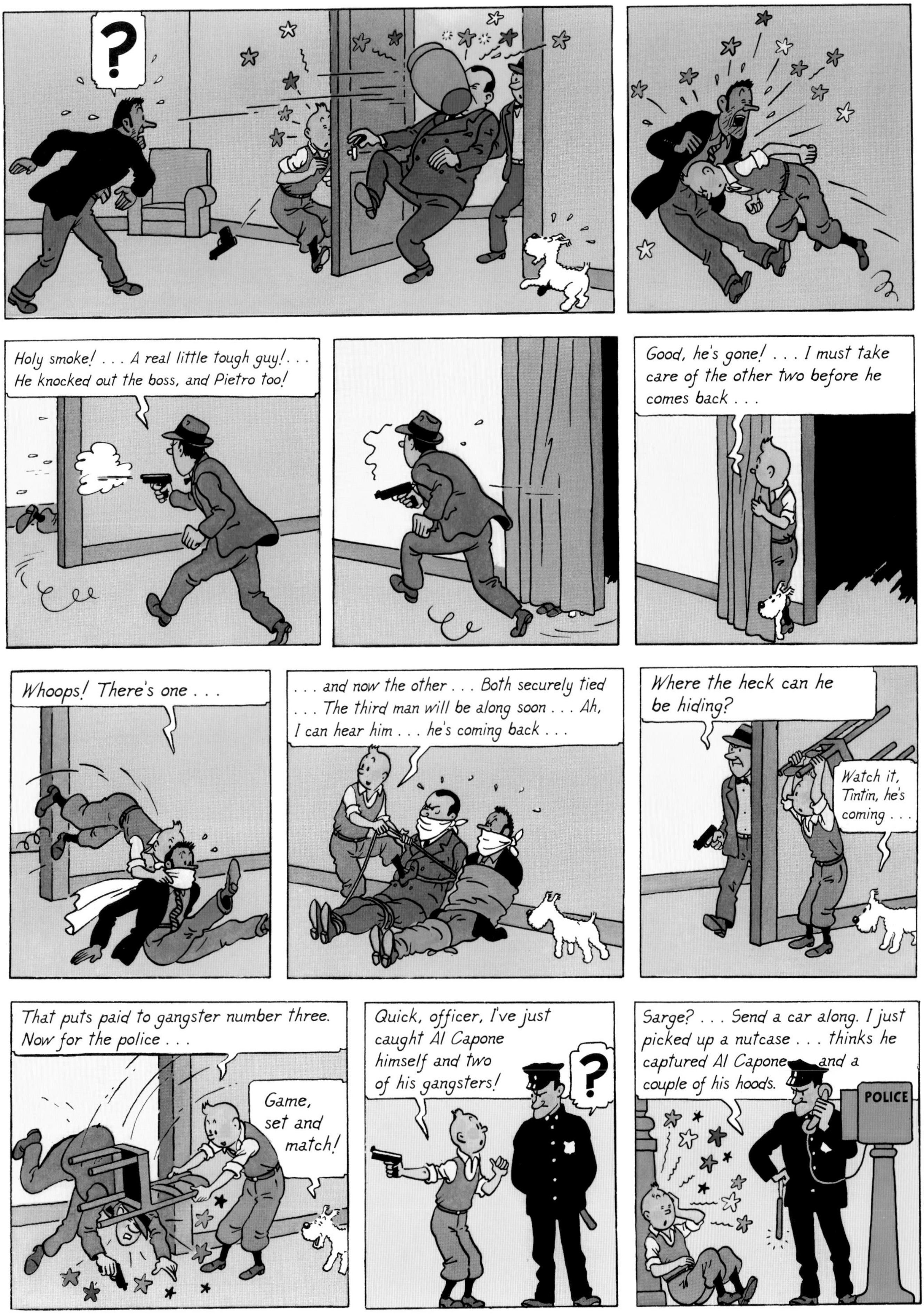
?
Holy smoke! . . . A real little tough guy! . . . He knocked out the boss, and Pietro too!
Good, he's gone! . . . I must take care of the other two before he comes back . . .
Whoops! There's one . . .
. . . and now the other . . . Both securely tied . . . The third man will be along soon . . . Ah, I can hear him . . . he's coming back . . .
Where the heck can he be hiding?
Watch it, Tintin, he's coming . . .
That puts paid to gangster number three. Now for the police . . .
Game, set and match!
Quick, officer, I've just caught Al Capone himself and two of his gangsters!
?
Sarge? . . . Send a car along. I just picked up a nutcase . . . thinks he captured Al Capone . . . and a couple of his hoods.
POLICE

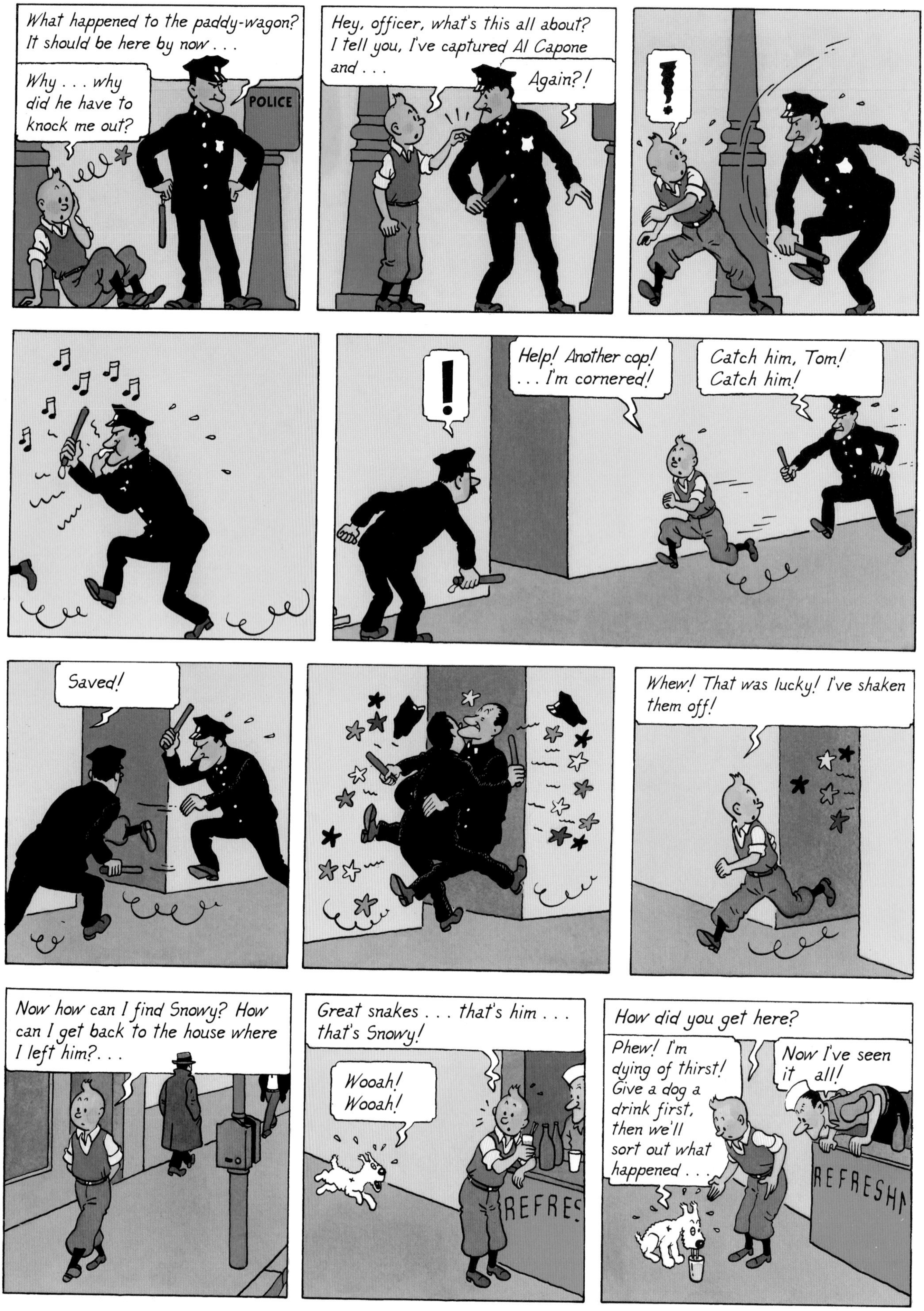
What happened to the paddy-wagon? It should be here by now . . .
Why . . . why did he have to knock me out?
POLICE
Hey, officer, what's this all about? I tell you, I've captured Al Capone and . . .
Again?!
!
Help! Another cop! . . . I'm cornered!
Catch him, Tom! Catch him!
!
Saved!
Whew! That was lucky! I've shaken them off!
Now how can I find Snowy? How can I get back to the house where I left him? . . .
Great snakes . . . that's him . . . that's Snowy!
Wooah! Wooah!
REFRES
How did you get here?
Phew! I'm dying of thirst! Give a dog a drink first, then we'll sort out what happened . . .
Now I've seen it all!
REFRESHM

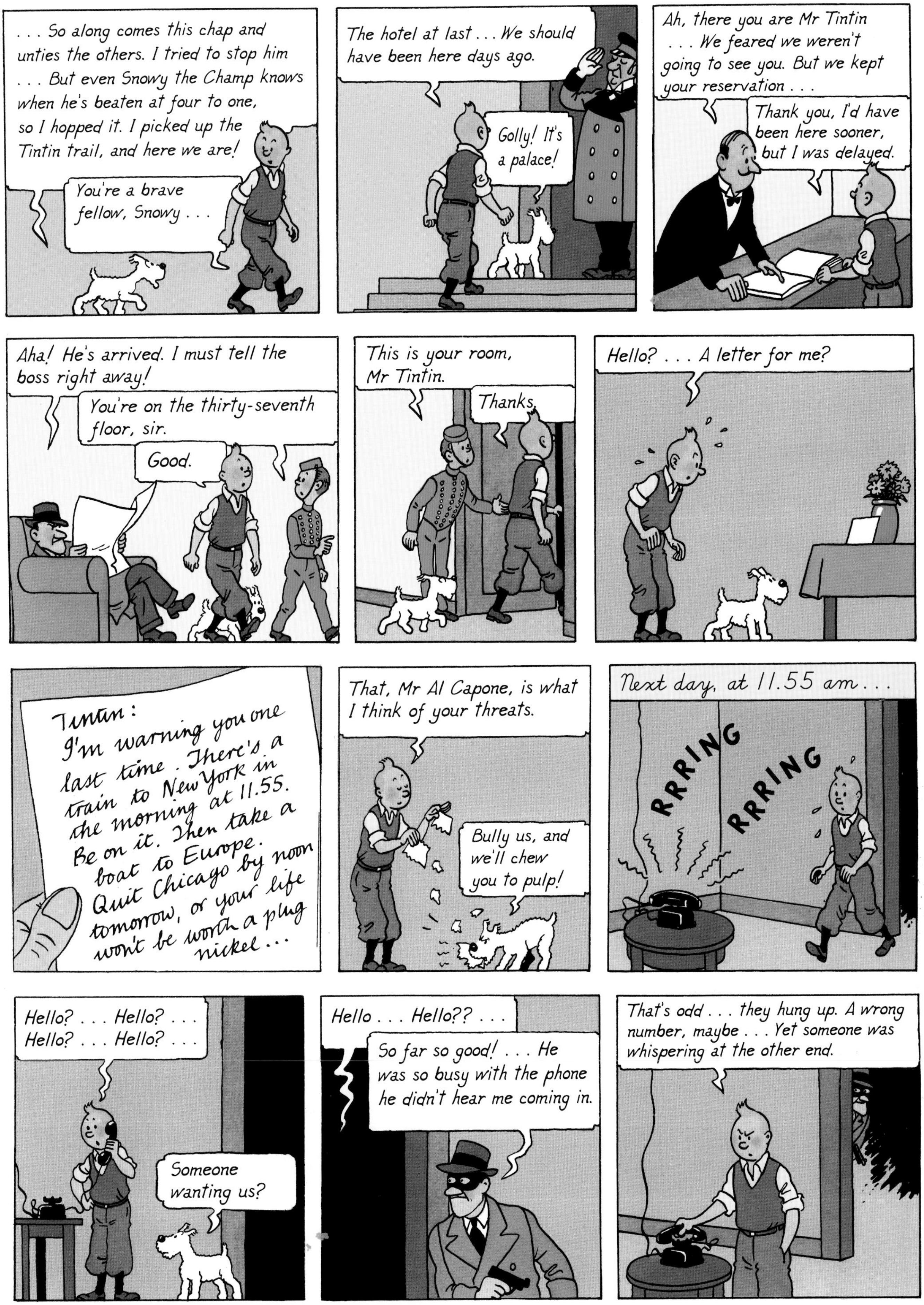

. . . So along comes this chap and unties the others. I tried to stop him . . . But even Snowy the Champ knows when he's beaten at four to one, so I hopped it. I picked up the Tintin trail, and here we are!
You're a brave fellow, Snowy . . .
The hotel at last . . . We should have been here days ago.
Golly! It's a palace!
Ah, there you are Mr Tintin . . . We feared we weren't going to see you. But we kept your reservation . . .
Thank you, I'd have been here sooner, but I was delayed.
Aha! He's arrived. I must tell the boss right away!
You're on the thirty-seventh floor, sir.
Good.
This is your room, Mr Tintin.
Thanks.
Hello? . . . A letter for me?
Tintin:
I'm warning you one last time. There's a train to New York in the morning at 11.55. Be on it. Then take a boat to Europe. Quit Chicago by noon tomorrow, or your life won't be worth a plug nickel . . .
That, Mr Al Capone, is what I think of your threats.
Bully us, and we'll chew you to pulp!
Next day, at 11.55 am . . .
RRRING
RRRING
Hello? . . . Hello? . . . Hello? . . . Hello? . . .
Someone wanting us?
Hello . . . Hello?? . . .
So far so good! . . . He was so busy with the phone he didn't hear me coming in.
That's odd . . . they hung up. A wrong number, maybe . . . Yet someone was whispering at the other end.

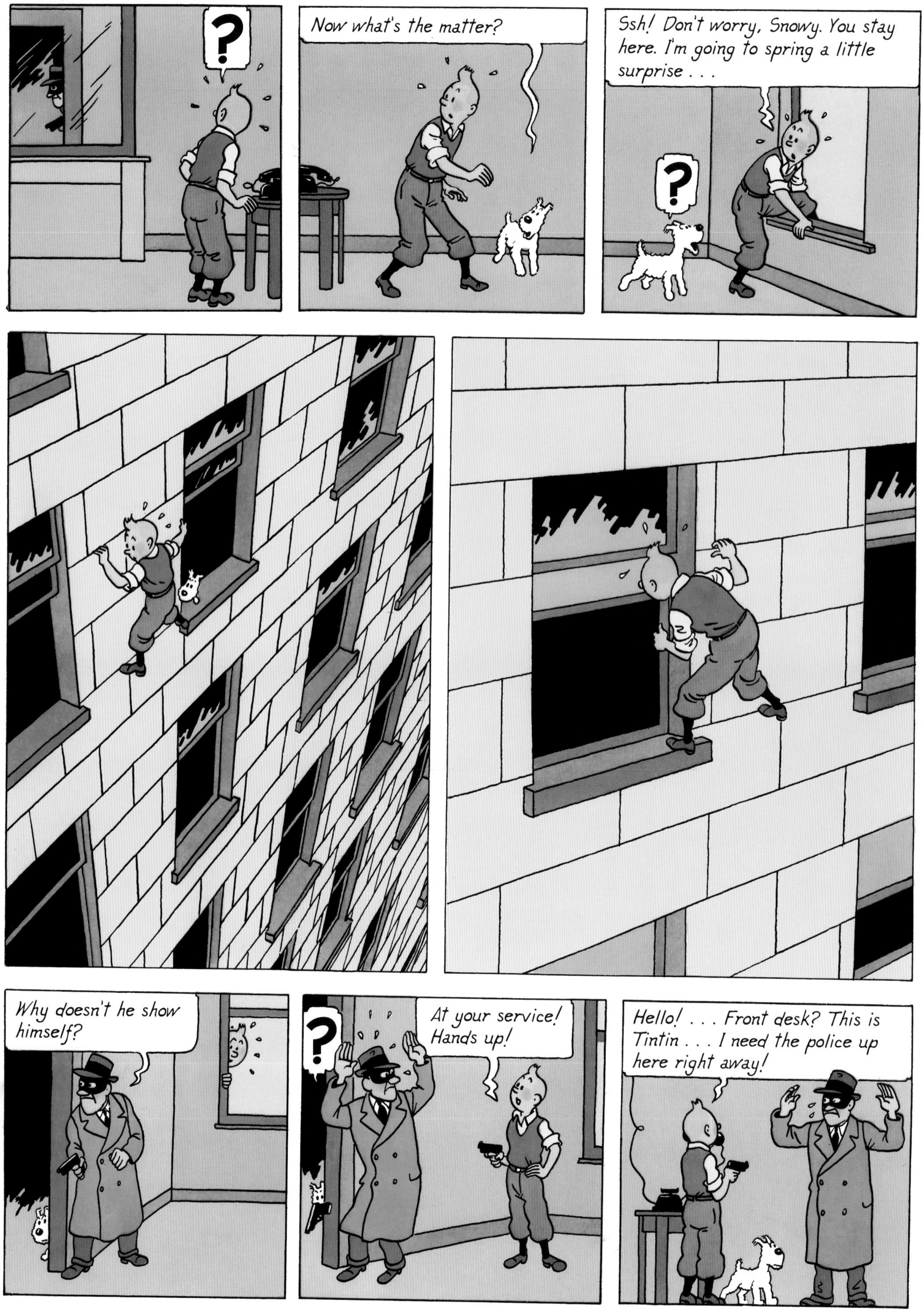
?
Now what's the matter?
Ssh! Don't worry, Snowy. You stay here. I'm going to spring a little surprise . . .
?
Why doesn't he show himself?
?
At your service! Hands up!
Hello! . . . Front desk? This is Tintin . . . I need the police up here right away!

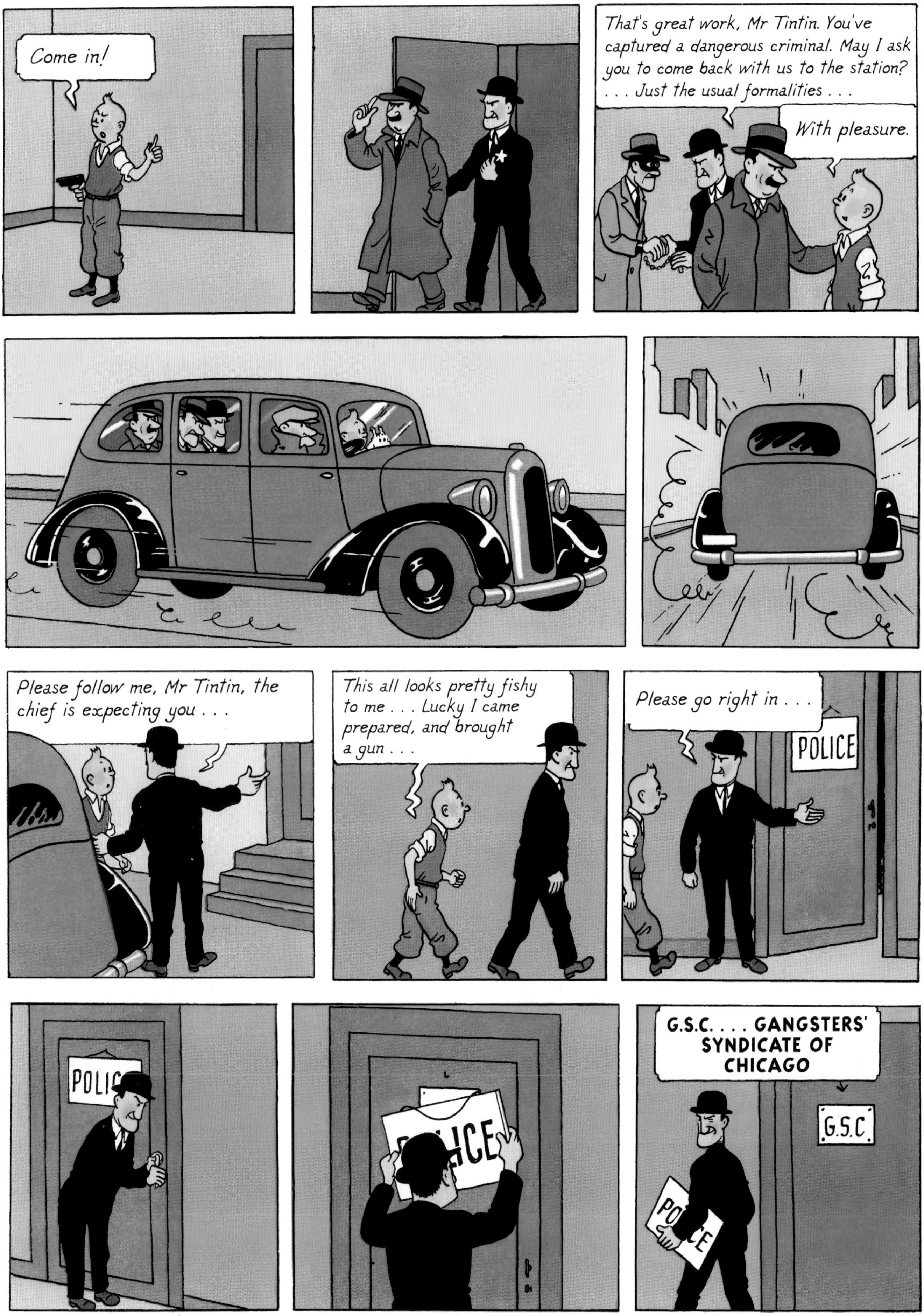
Come in!
That's great work, Mr Tintin. You've captured a dangerous criminal. May I ask you to come back with us to the station? . . . Just the usual formalities . . .
With pleasure.
Please follow me, Mr Tintin, the chief is expecting you . . .
This all looks pretty fishy to me . . . Lucky I came prepared, and brought a gun . . .
Please go right in . . .
POLICE
POLIC
POLICE
G.S.C. . . . GANGSTERS' SYNDICATE OF CHICAGO
G.S.C.

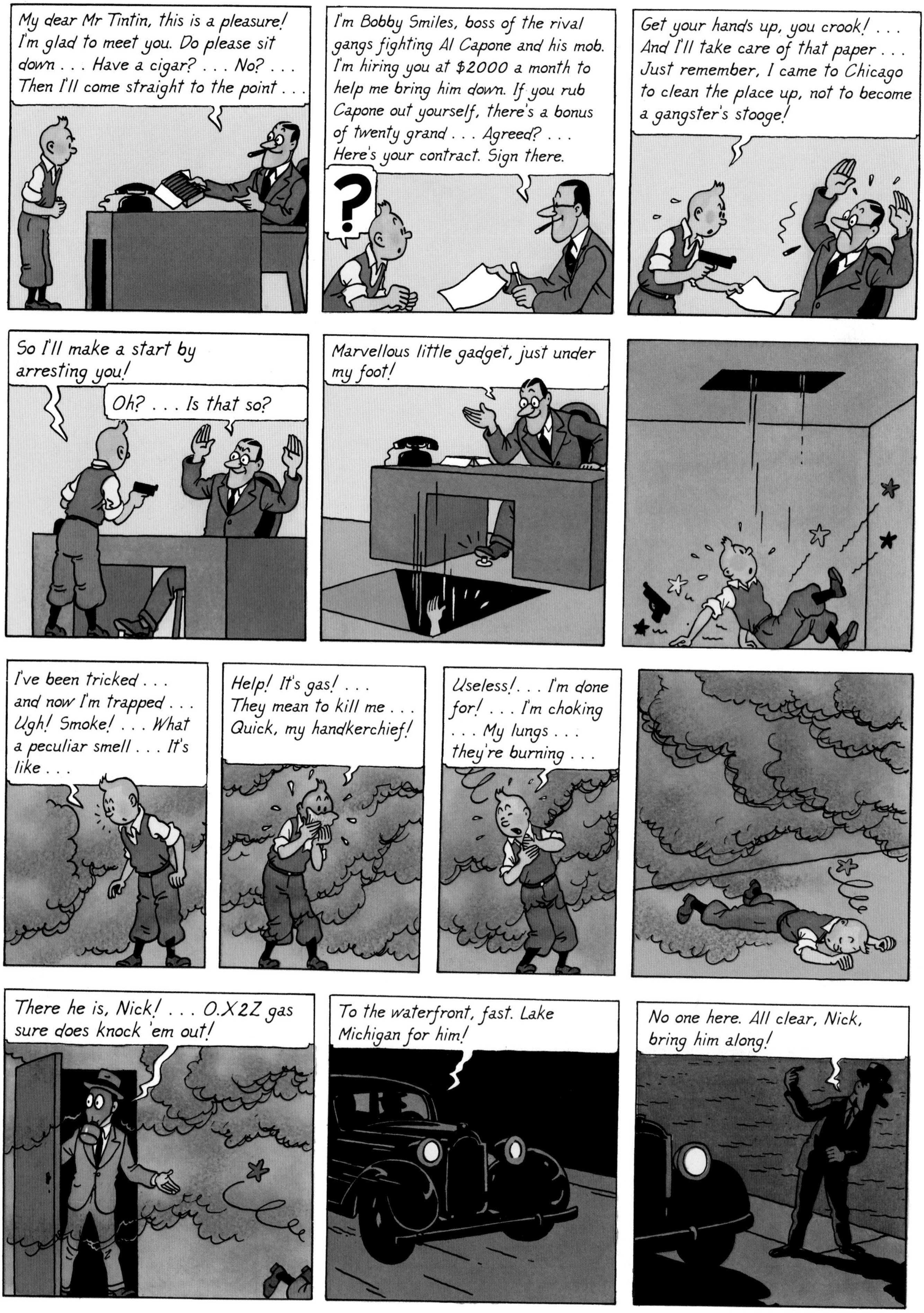
My dear Mr Tintin, this is a pleasure! I'm glad to meet you. Do please sit down . . . Have a cigar? . . . No? . . . Then I'll come straight to the point . . .
I'm Bobby Smiles, boss of the rival gangs fighting Al Capone and his mob. I'm hiring you at $2000 a month to help me bring him down. If you rub Capone out yourself, there's a bonus of twenty grand . . . Agreed? . . . Here's your contract. Sign there.
?
Get your hands up, you crook! . . . And I'll take care of that paper . . . Just remember, I came to Chicago to clean the place up, not to become a gangster's stooge!
So I'll make a start by arresting you!
Oh? . . . Is that so?
Marvellous little gadget, just under my foot!
I've been tricked . . . and now I'm trapped . . . Ugh! Smoke! . . . What a peculiar smell . . . It's like . . .
Help! It's gas! . . . They mean to kill me . . . Quick, my handkerchief!
Useless! . . . I'm done for! . . . I'm choking . . . My lungs . . . they're burning . . .
There he is, Nick! . . . O.X2Z gas sure does knock 'em out!
To the waterfront, fast. Lake Michigan for him!
No one here. All clear, Nick, bring him along!

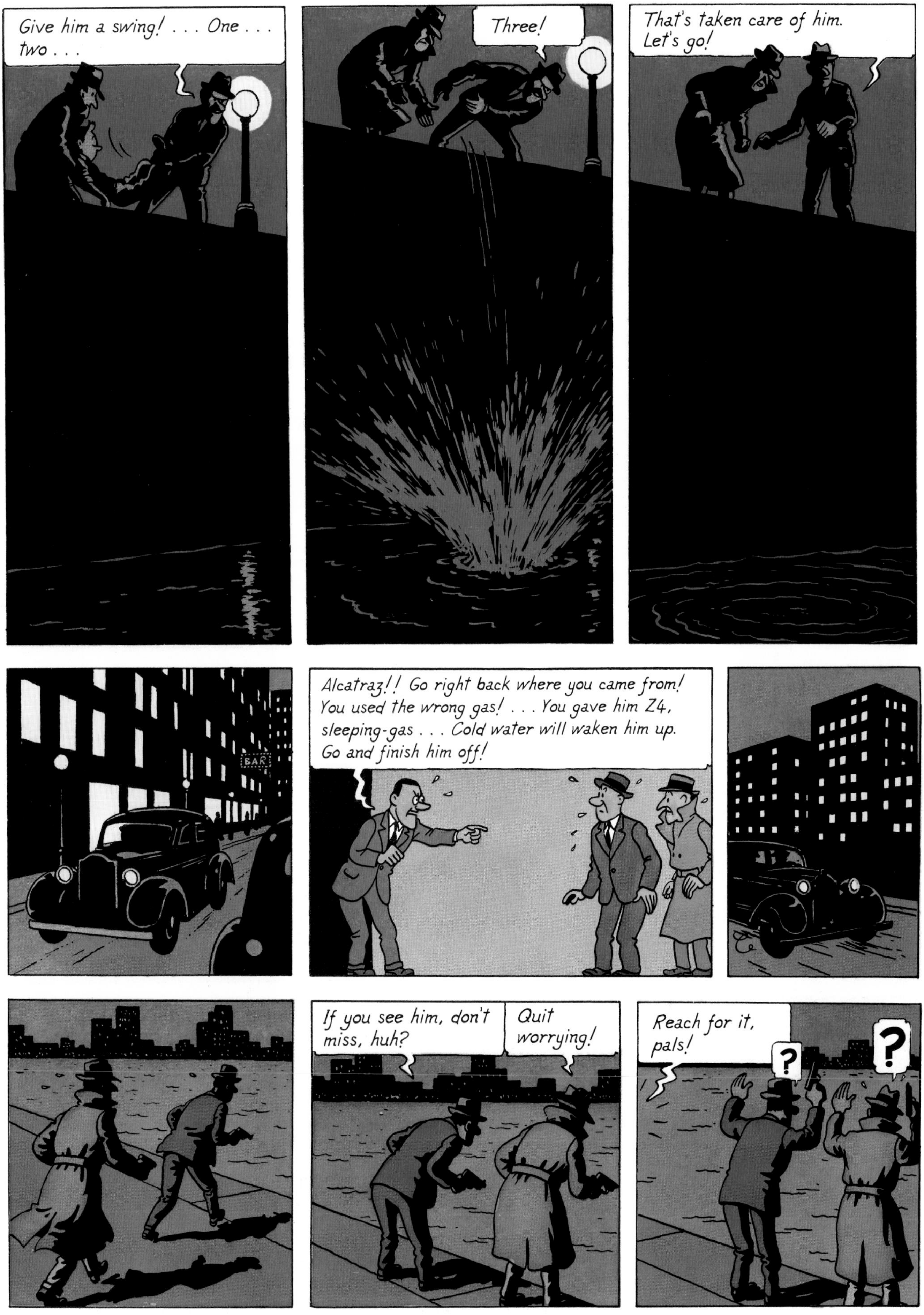
Give him a swing! . . . One . . . two . . .
Three!
That's taken care of him. Let's go!
BAR
Alcatraz!! Go right back where you came from! You used the wrong gas! . . . You gave him Z4, sleeping-gas . . . Cold water will waken him up. Go and finish him off!
If you see him, don't miss, huh?
Quit worrying!
Reach for it, pals!
?
?

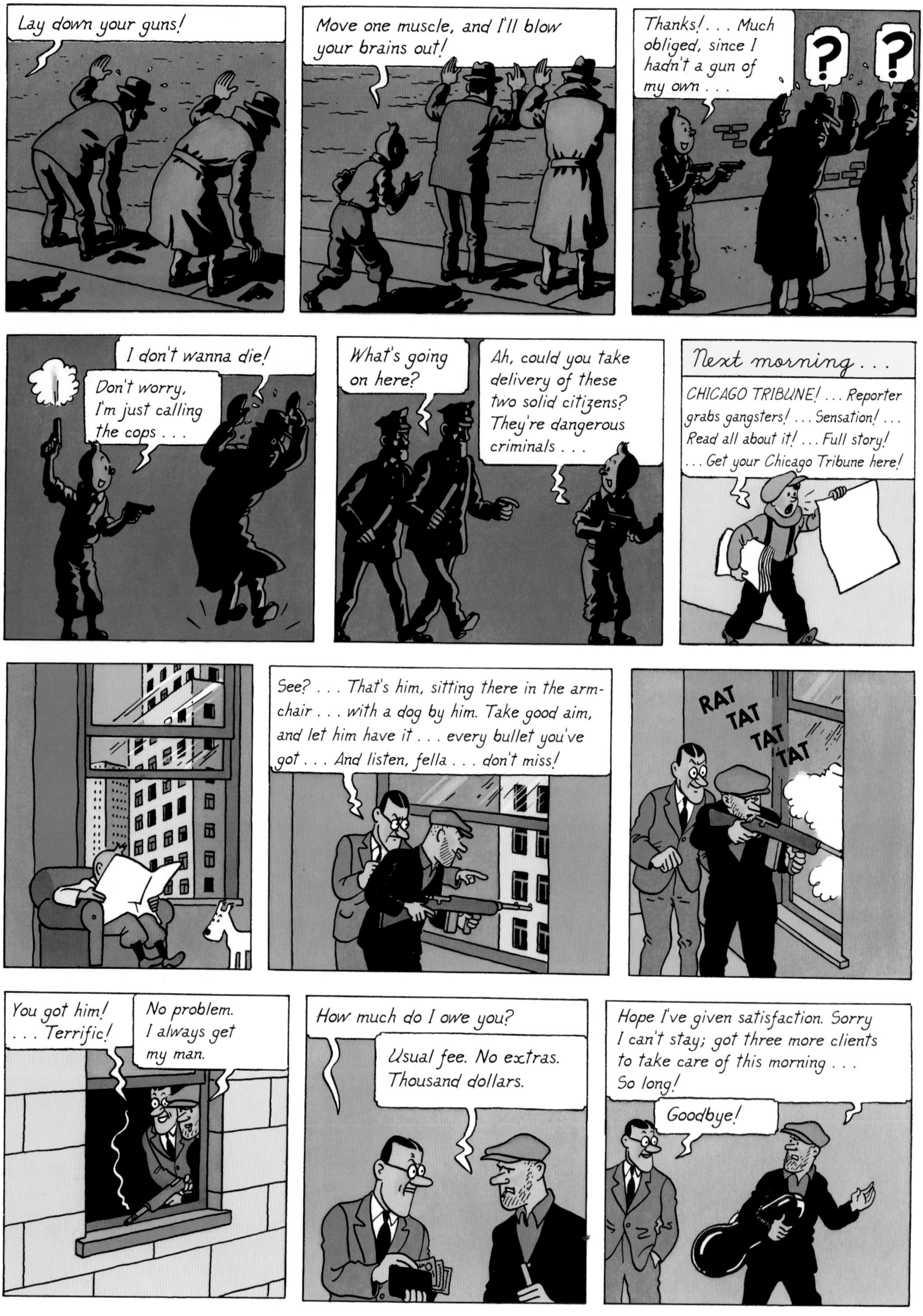
Lay down your guns!
Move one muscle, and I'll blow your brains out!
Thanks! . . . Much obliged, since I hadn't a gun of my own . . .
?
?
I don't wanna die!
Don't worry, I'm just calling the cops . . .
What's going on here?
Ah, could you take delivery of these two solid citizens? They're dangerous criminals . . .
Next morning . . .
CHICAGO TRIBUNE! . . . Reporter grabs gangsters! . . . Sensation! . . . Read all about it! . . . Full story! . . . Get your Chicago Tribune here!
See? . . . That's him, sitting there in the arm-chair . . . with a dog by him. Take good aim, and let him have it . . . every bullet you've got . . . And listen, fella . . . don't miss!
RAT TAT TAT TAT
You got him! . . . Terrific!
No problem. I always get my man.
How much do I owe you?
Usual fee. No extras. Thousand dollars.
Hope I've given satisfaction. Sorry I can't stay; got three more clients to take care of this morning . . . So long!
Goodbye!

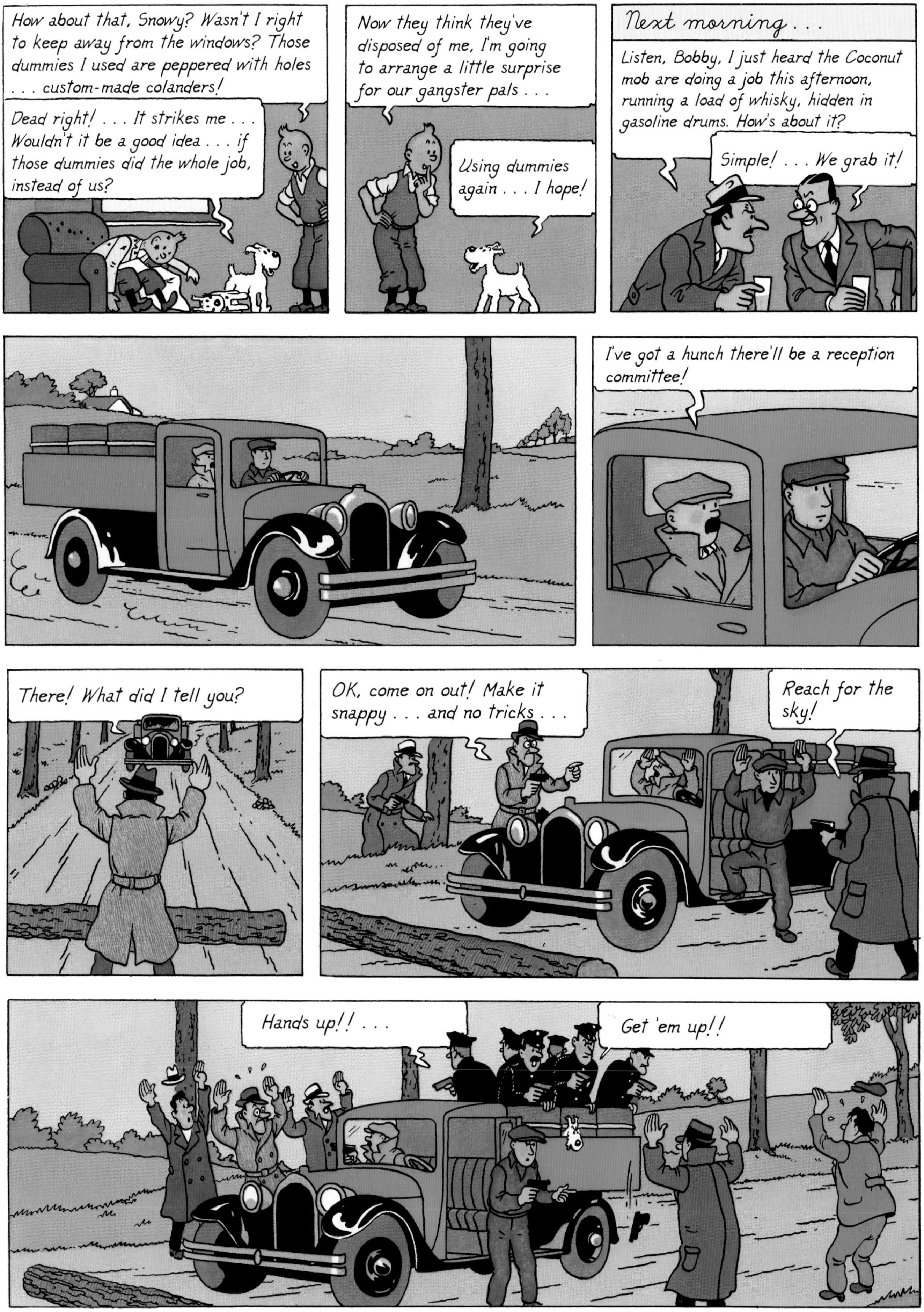

How about that, Snowy? Wasn't I right to keep away from the windows? Those dummies I used are peppered with holes . . . custom-made colanders!
Dead right! . . . It strikes me . . . Wouldn't it be a good idea . . . if those dummies did the whole job, instead of us?
Now they think they've disposed of me, I'm going to arrange a little surprise for our gangster pals . . .
Using dummies again . . . I hope!
Next morning . . .
Listen, Bobby, I just heard the Coconut mob are doing a job this afternoon, running a load of whisky, hidden in gasoline drums. How's about it?
Simple! . . . We grab it!
I've got a hunch there'll be a reception committee!
There! What did I tell you?
OK, come on out! Make it snappy . . . and no tricks . . .
Reach for the sky!
Hands up!! . . .
Get 'em up!!

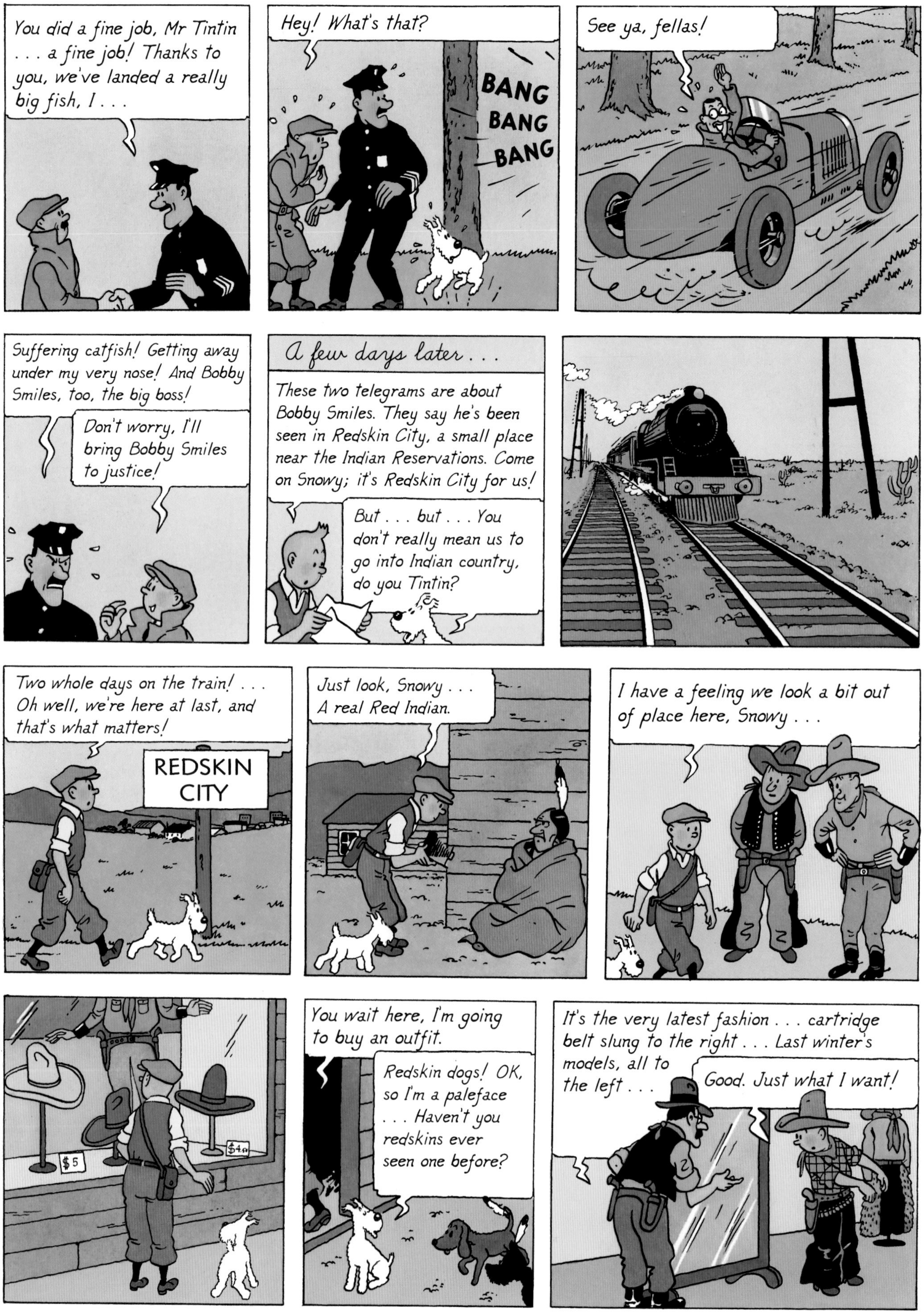

You did a fine job, Mr Tintin . . . a fine job! Thanks to you, we've landed a really big fish, I . . .
Hey! What's that?
BANG
BANG
BANG
See ya, fellas!
Suffering catfish! Getting away under my very nose! And Bobby Smiles, too, the big boss!
Don't worry, I'll bring Bobby Smiles to justice!
A few days later . . .
These two telegrams are about Bobby Smiles. They say he's been seen in Redskin City, a small place near the Indian Reservations. Come on Snowy; it's Redskin City for us!
But . . . but . . . You don't really mean us to go into Indian country, do you Tintin?
Two whole days on the train! . . . Oh well, we're here at last, and that's what matters!
REDSKIN CITY
Just look, Snowy . . . A real Red Indian.
I have a feeling we look a bit out of place here, Snowy . . .
$5
You wait here, I'm going to buy an outfit.
Redskin dogs! OK, so I'm a paleface . . . Haven't you redskins ever seen one before?
It's the very latest fashion . . . cartridge belt slung to the right . . . Last winter's models, all to the left . . .
Good. Just what I want!

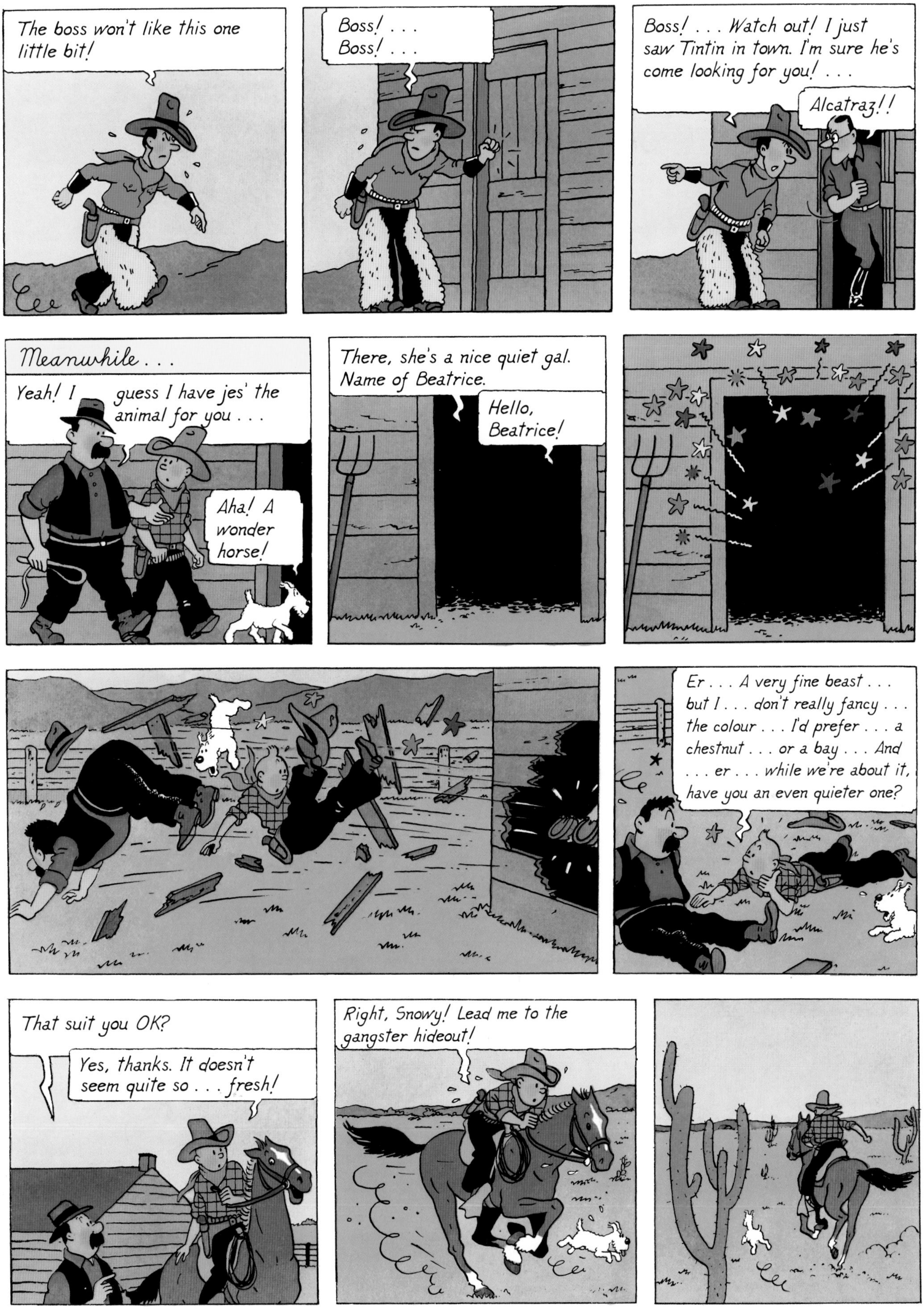
The boss won't like this one little bit!
Boss! . . . Boss! . . .
Boss! . . . Watch out! I just saw Tintin in town. I'm sure he's come looking for you! . . .
Alcatraz!!
Meanwhile . . .
Yeah! I guess I have jes' the animal for you . . .
Aha! A wonder horse!
There, she's a nice quiet gal. Name of Beatrice.
Hello, Beatrice!
Er . . . A very fine beast . . . but I . . . don't really fancy . . . the colour . . . I'd prefer . . . a chestnut . . . or a bay . . . And . . . er . . . while we're about it, have you an even quieter one?
That suit you OK?
Yes, thanks. It doesn't seem quite so . . . fresh!
Right, Snowy! Lead me to the gangster hideout!

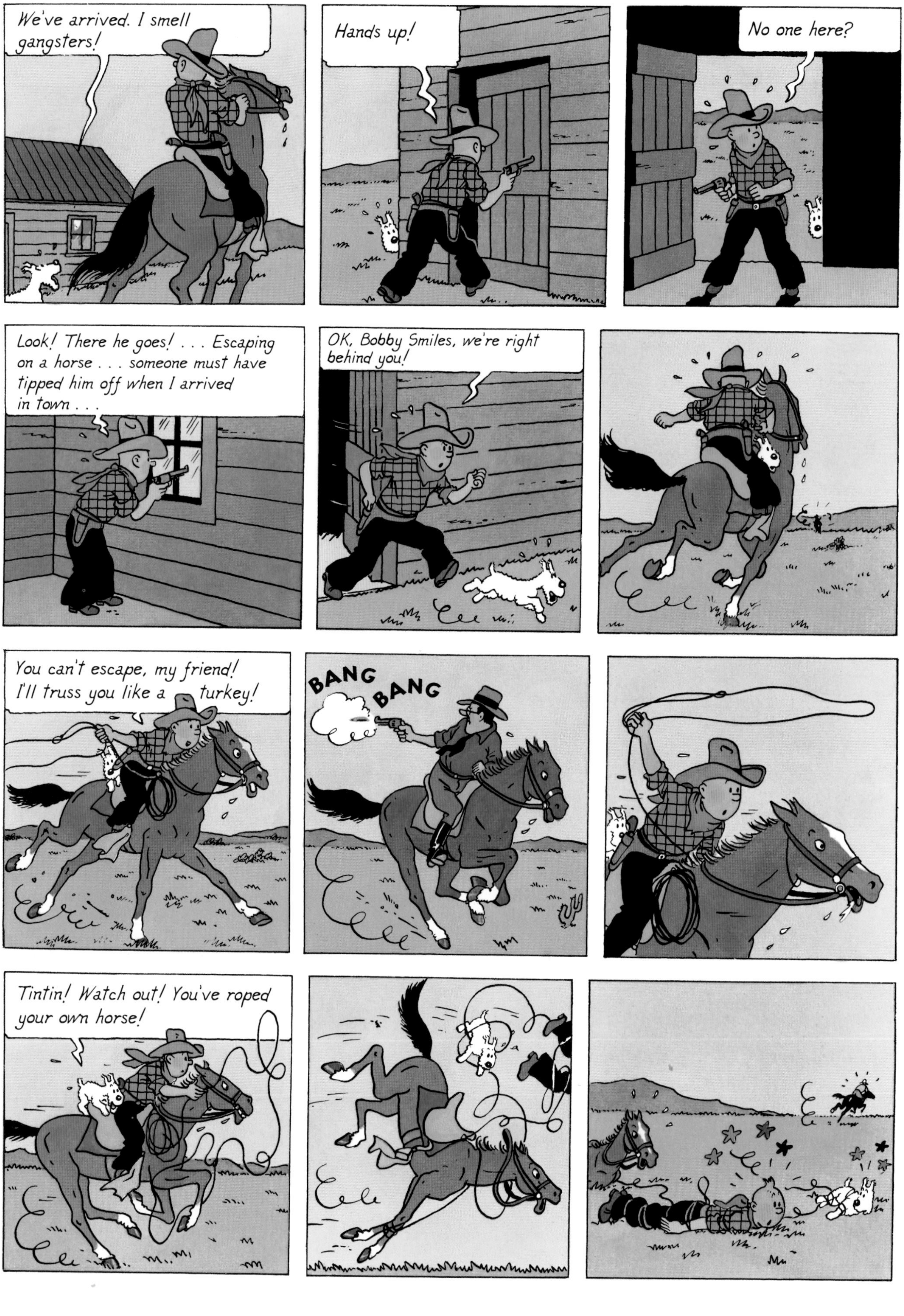
We've arrived. I smell gangsters!
Hands up!
No one here?
Look! There he goes! . . . Escaping on a horse . . . someone must have tipped him off when I arrived in town . . .
OK, Bobby Smiles, we're right behind you!
You can't escape, my friend! I'll truss you like a turkey!
BANG
BANG
Tintin! Watch out! You've roped your own horse!

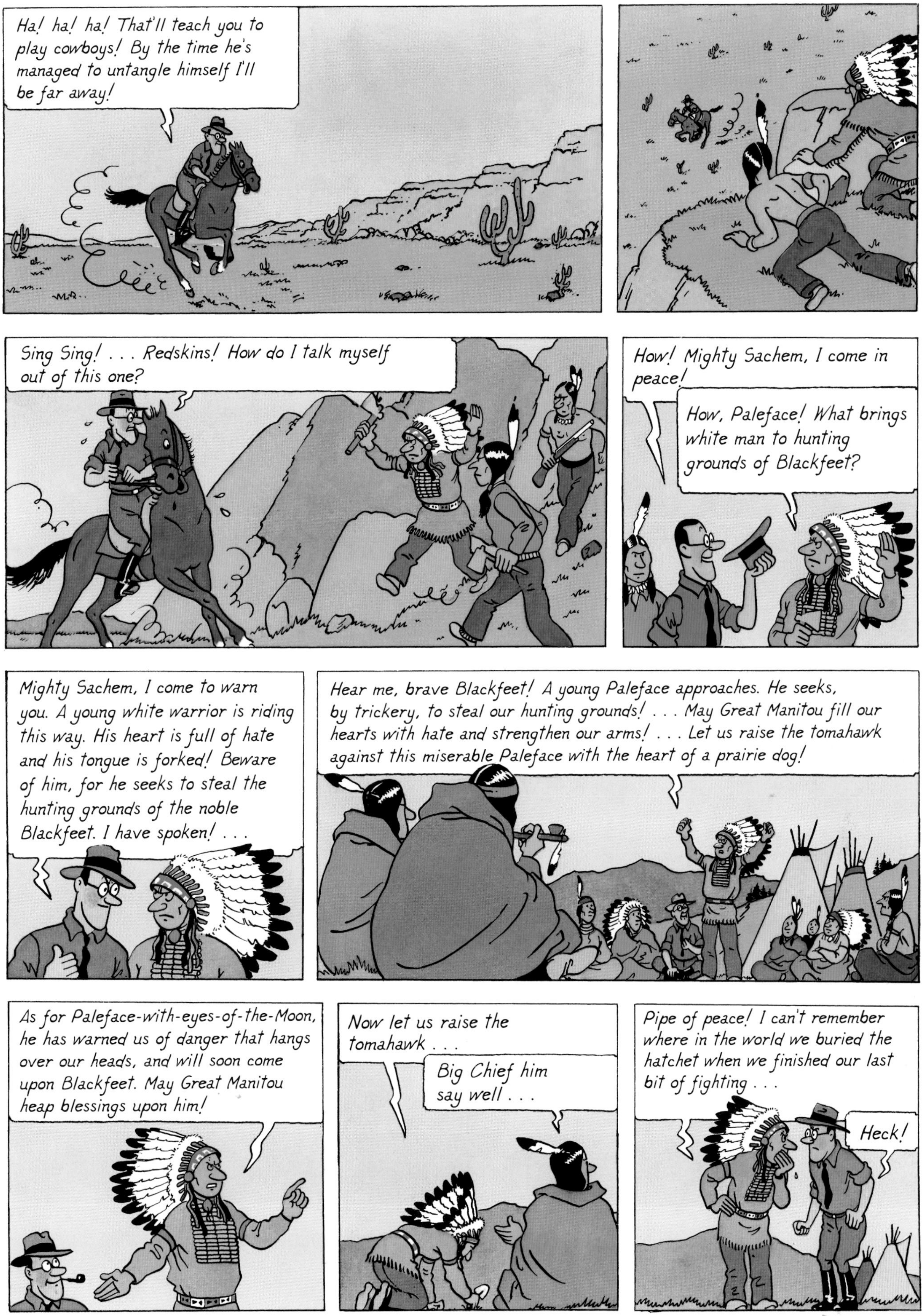

Ha! ha! ha! That'll teach you to play cowboys! By the time he's managed to untangle himself I'll be far away!
Sing Sing! . . . Redskins! How do I talk myself out of this one?
How! Mighty Sachem, I come in peace!
How, Paleface! What brings white man to hunting grounds of Blackfeet?
Mighty Sachem, I come to warn you. A young white warrior is riding this way. His heart is full of hate and his tongue is forked! Beware of him, for he seeks to steal the hunting grounds of the noble Blackfeet. I have spoken! . . .
Hear me, brave Blackfeet! A young Paleface approaches. He seeks, by trickery, to steal our hunting grounds! . . . May Great Manitou fill our hearts with hate and strengthen our arms! . . . Let us raise the tomahawk against this miserable Paleface with the heart of a prairie dog!
As for Paleface-with-eyes-of-the-Moon, he has warned us of danger that hangs over our heads, and will soon come upon Blackfeet. May Great Manitou heap blessings upon him!
Now let us raise the tomahawk . . .
Big Chief him say well . . .
Pipe of peace! I can't remember where in the world we buried the hatchet when we finished our last bit of fighting . . .
Heck!

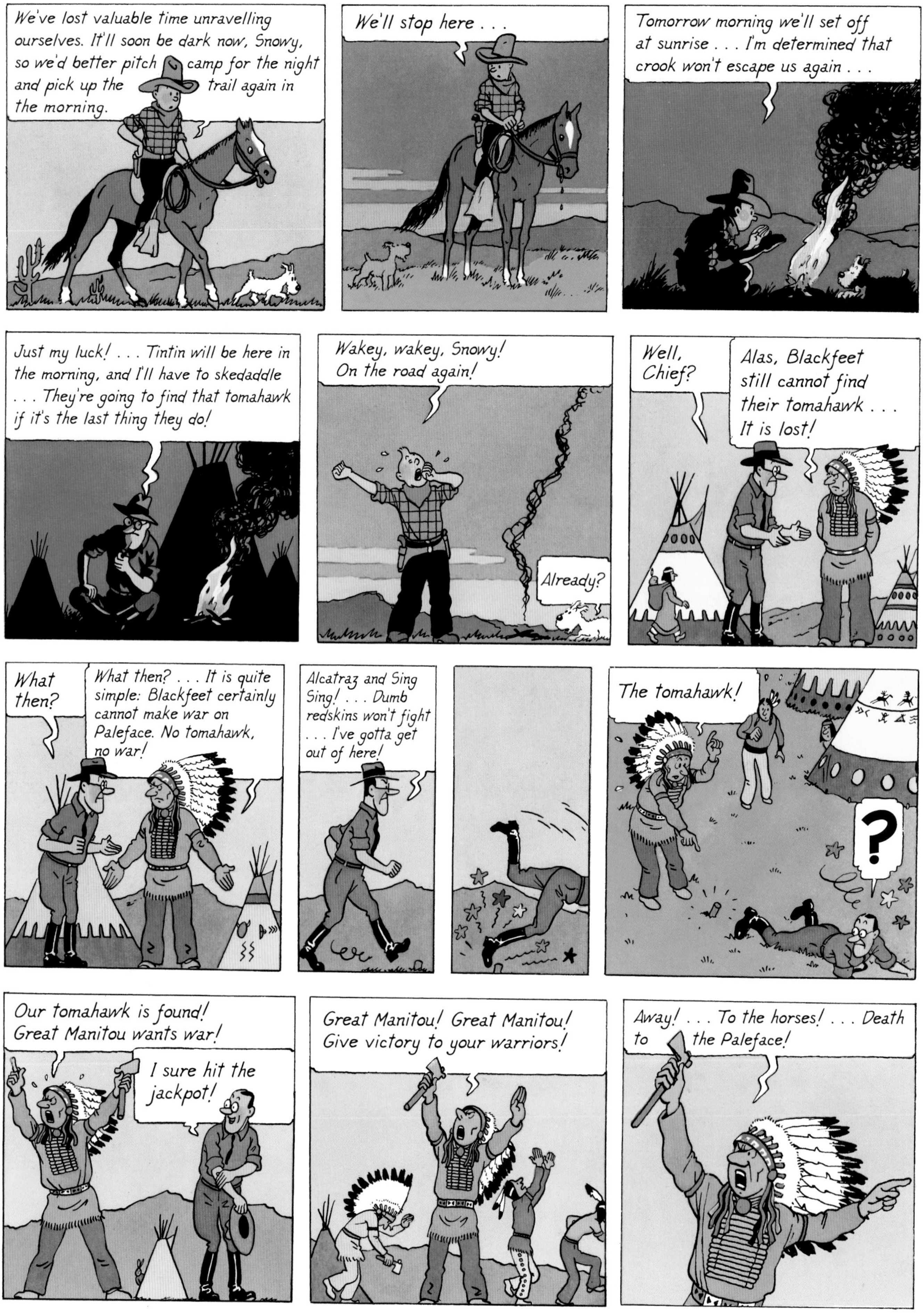
We've lost valuable time unravelling ourselves. It'll soon be dark now, Snowy, so we'd better pitch camp for the night and pick up the trail again in the morning.
We'll stop here . . .
Tomorrow morning we'll set off at sunrise . . . I'm determined that crook won't escape us again . . .
Just my luck! . . . Tintin will be here in the morning, and I'll have to skedaddle . . . They're going to find that tomahawk if it's the last thing they do!
Wakey, wakey, Snowy! On the road again!
Already?
Well, Chief?
Alas, Blackfeet still cannot find their tomahawk . . . It is lost!
What then?
What then? . . . It is quite simple: Blackfeet certainly cannot make war on Paleface. No tomahawk, no war!
Alcatraz and Sing Sing! . . . Dumb redskins won't fight . . . I've gotta get out of here!
The tomahawk!
?
Our tomahawk is found! Great Manitou wants war!
I sure hit the jackpot!
Great Manitou! Great Manitou! Give victory to your warriors!
Away! . . . To the horses! . . . Death to the Paleface!

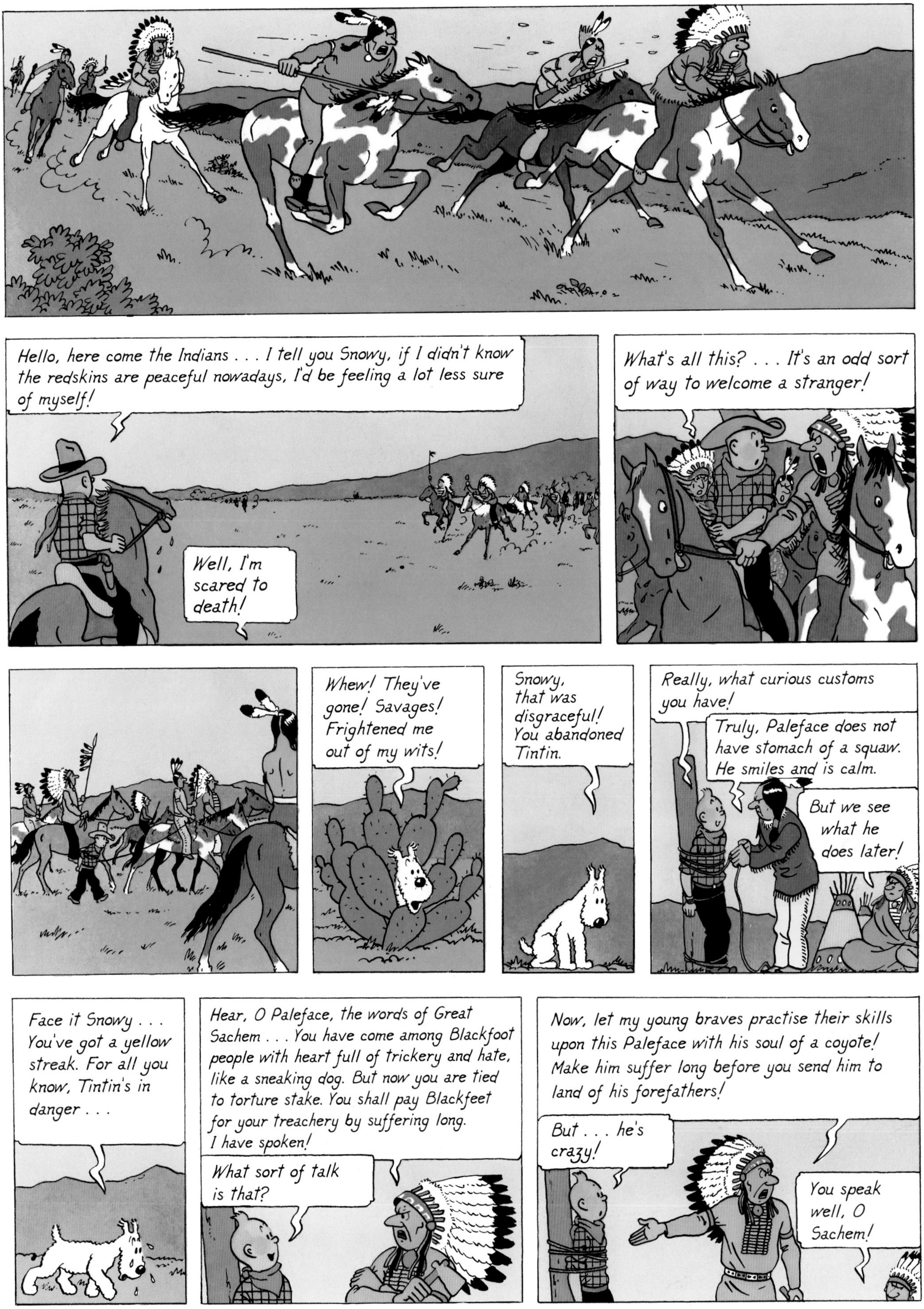
Hello, here come the Indians . . . I tell you Snowy, if I didn't know the redskins are peaceful nowadays, I'd be feeling a lot less sure of myself!
Well, I'm scared to death!
What's all this? . . . It's an odd sort of way to welcome a stranger!
Whew! They've gone! Savages! Frightened me out of my wits!
Snowy, that was disgraceful! You abandoned Tintin.
Really, what curious customs you have!
Truly, Paleface does not have stomach of a squaw. He smiles and is calm.
But we see what he does later!
Face it Snowy . . . You've got a yellow streak. For all you know, Tintin's in danger . . .
Hear, O Paleface, the words of Great Sachem . . . You have come among Blackfoot people with heart full of trickery and hate, like a sneaking dog. But now you are tied to torture stake. You shall pay Blackfeet for your treachery by suffering long. I have spoken!
What sort of talk is that?
Now, let my young braves practise their skills upon this Paleface with his soul of a coyote! Make him suffer long before you send him to land of his forefathers!
But . . . he's crazy!
You speak well, O Sachem!

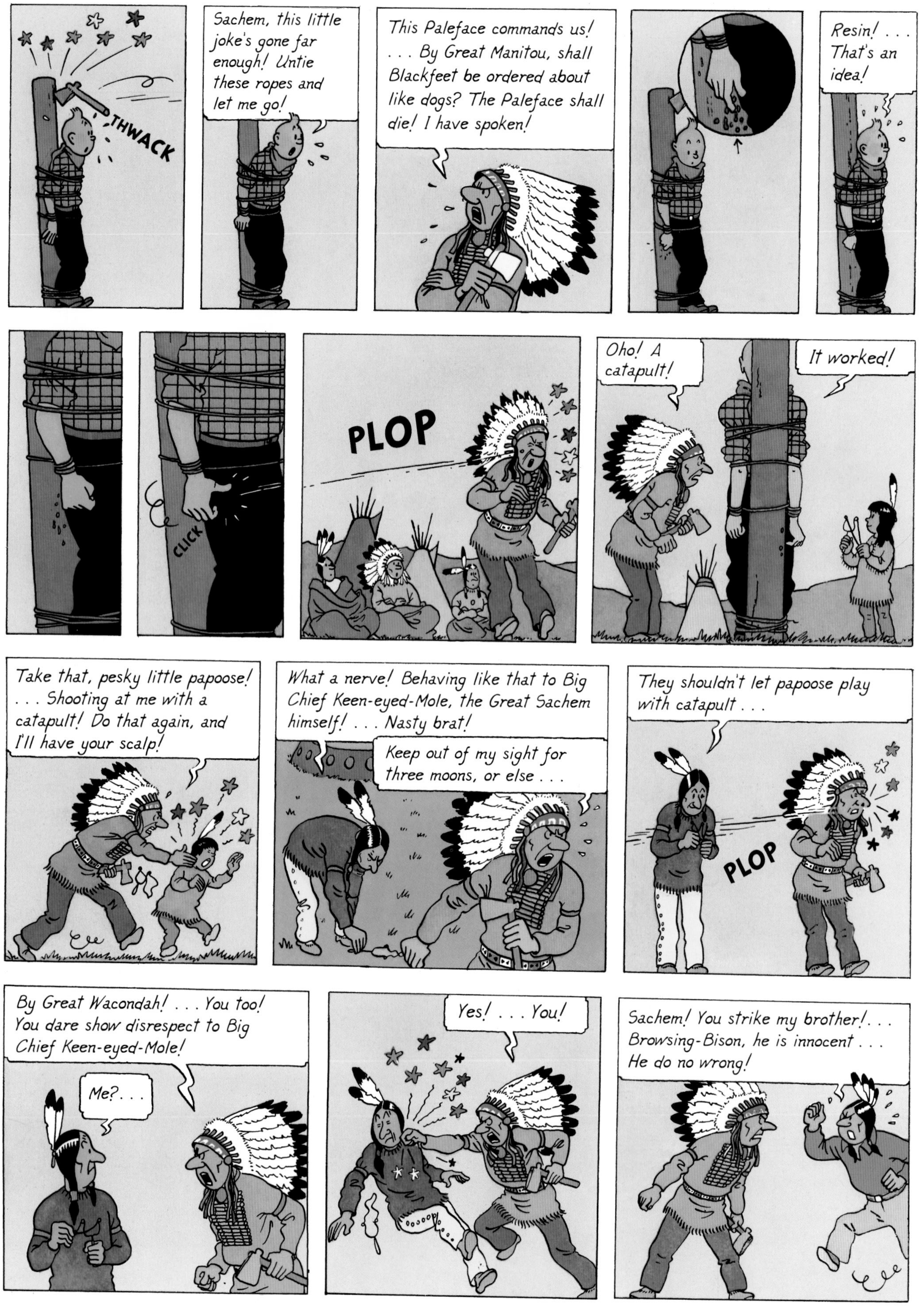
THWACK
Sachem, this little joke's gone far enough! Untie these ropes and let me go!
This Paleface commands us! . . . By Great Manitou, shall Blackfeet be ordered about like dogs? The Paleface shall die! I have spoken!
Resin! . . . That's an idea!
CLICK
PLOP
Oho! A catapult!
It worked!
Take that, pesky little papoose! . . . Shooting at me with a catapult! Do that again, and I'll have your scalp!
What a nerve! Behaving like that to Big Chief Keen-eyed-Mole, the Great Sachem himself! . . . Nasty brat!
Keep out of my sight for three moons, or else . . .
They shouldn't let papoose play with catapult . . .
PLOP
By Great Wacondah! . . . You too! You dare show disrespect to Big Chief Keen-eyed-Mole!
Me? . . .
Yes! . . . You!
Sachem! You strike my brother! . . . Browsing-Bison, he is innocent . . . He do no wrong!

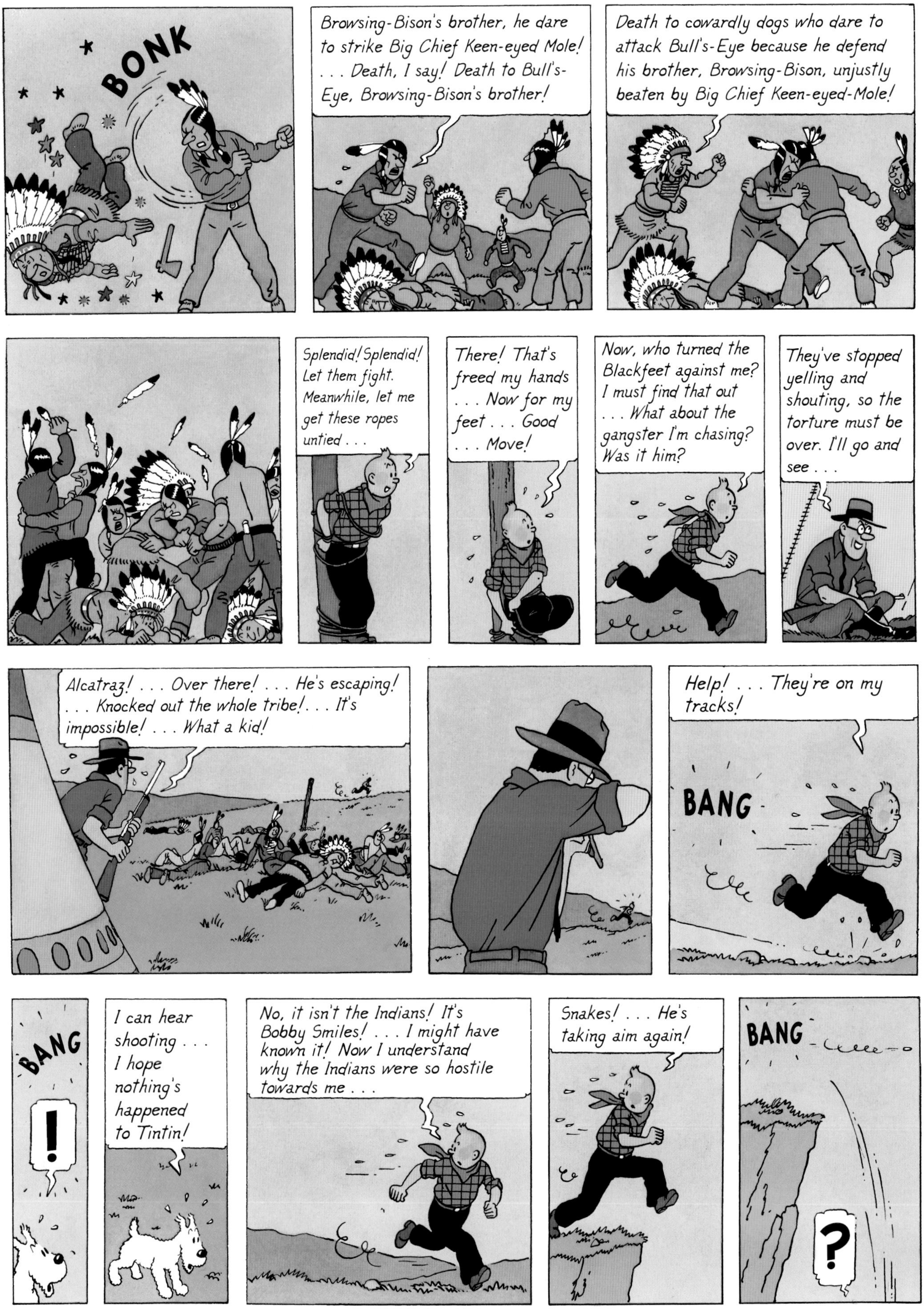
BONK
Browsing-Bison's brother, he dare to strike Big Chief Keen-eyed Mole! . . . Death, I say! Death to Bull's-Eye, Browsing-Bison's brother!
Death to cowardly dogs who dare to attack Bull's-Eye because he defend his brother, Browsing-Bison, unjustly beaten by Big Chief Keen-eyed-Mole!
Splendid! Splendid! Let them fight. Meanwhile, let me get these ropes untied . . .
There! That's freed my hands . . . Now for my feet . . . Good . . . Move!
Now, who turned the Blackfeet against me? I must find that out . . . What about the gangster I'm chasing? Was it him?
They've stopped yelling and shouting, so the torture must be over. I'll go and see . . .
Alcatraz! . . . Over there! . . . He's escaping! . . . Knocked out the whole tribe! . . . It's impossible! . . . What a kid!
Help! . . . They're on my tracks!
BANG
BANG
!
I can hear shooting . . . I hope nothing's happened to Tintin!
No, it isn't the Indians! It's Bobby Smiles! . . . I might have known it! Now I understand why the Indians were so hostile towards me . . .
Snakes! . . . He's taking aim again!
BANG
?

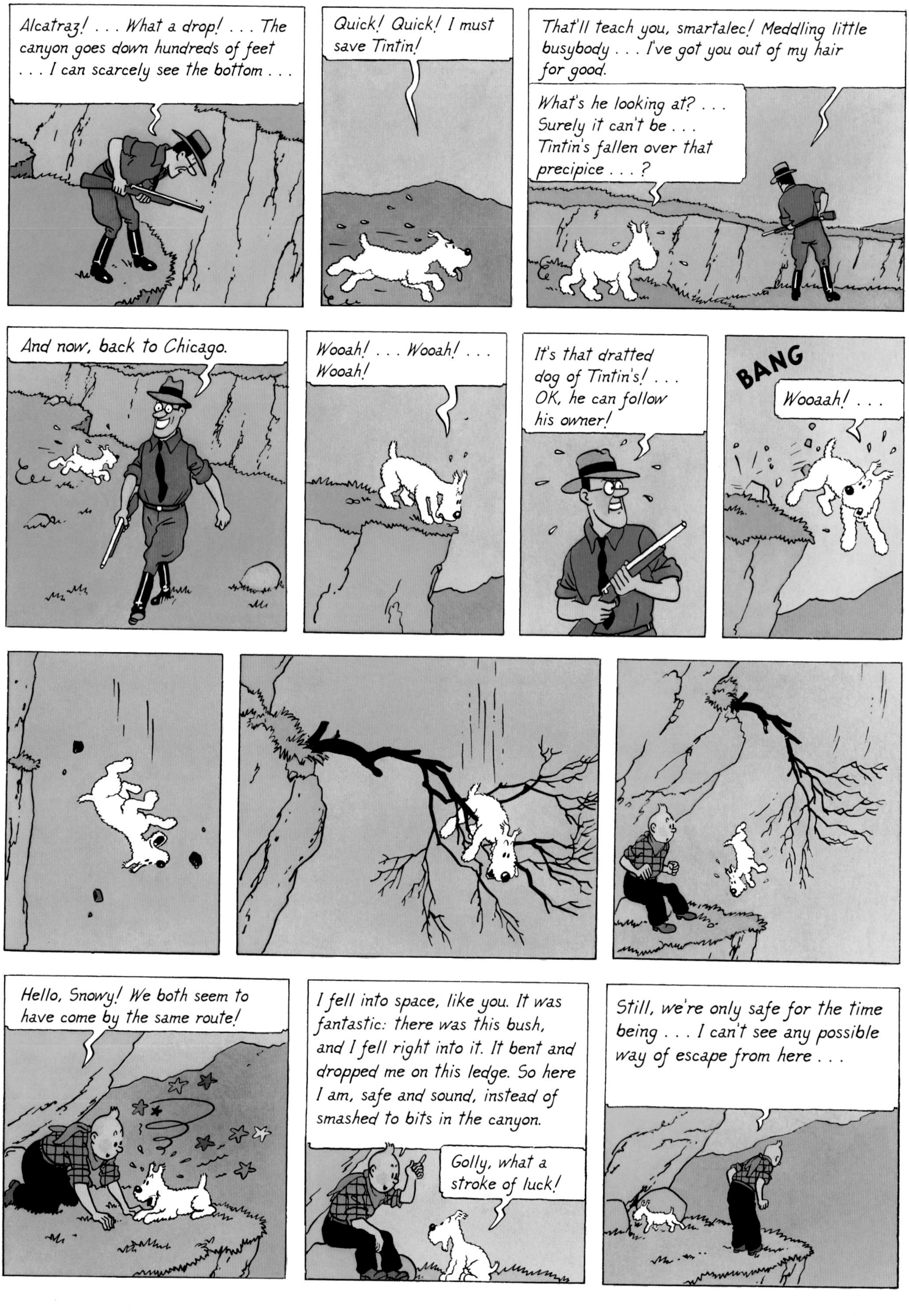
Alcatraz! . . . What a drop! . . . The canyon goes down hundreds of feet . . . I can scarcely see the bottom . . .
Quick! Quick! I must save Tintin!
That'll teach you, smartalec! Meddling little busybody . . . I've got you out of my hair for good.
What's he looking at? . . . Surely it can't be . . . Tintin's fallen over that precipice . . . ?
And now, back to Chicago.
Wooah! . . . Wooah! . . . Wooah!
It's that dratted dog of Tintin's! . . . OK, he can follow his owner!
BANG
Wooaah! . . .
Hello, Snowy! We both seem to have come by the same route!
I fell into space, like you. It was fantastic: there was this bush, and I fell right into it. It bent and dropped me on this ledge. So here I am, safe and sound, instead of smashed to bits in the canyon.
Golly, what a stroke of luck!
Still, we're only safe for the time being . . . I can't see any possible way of escape from here . . .

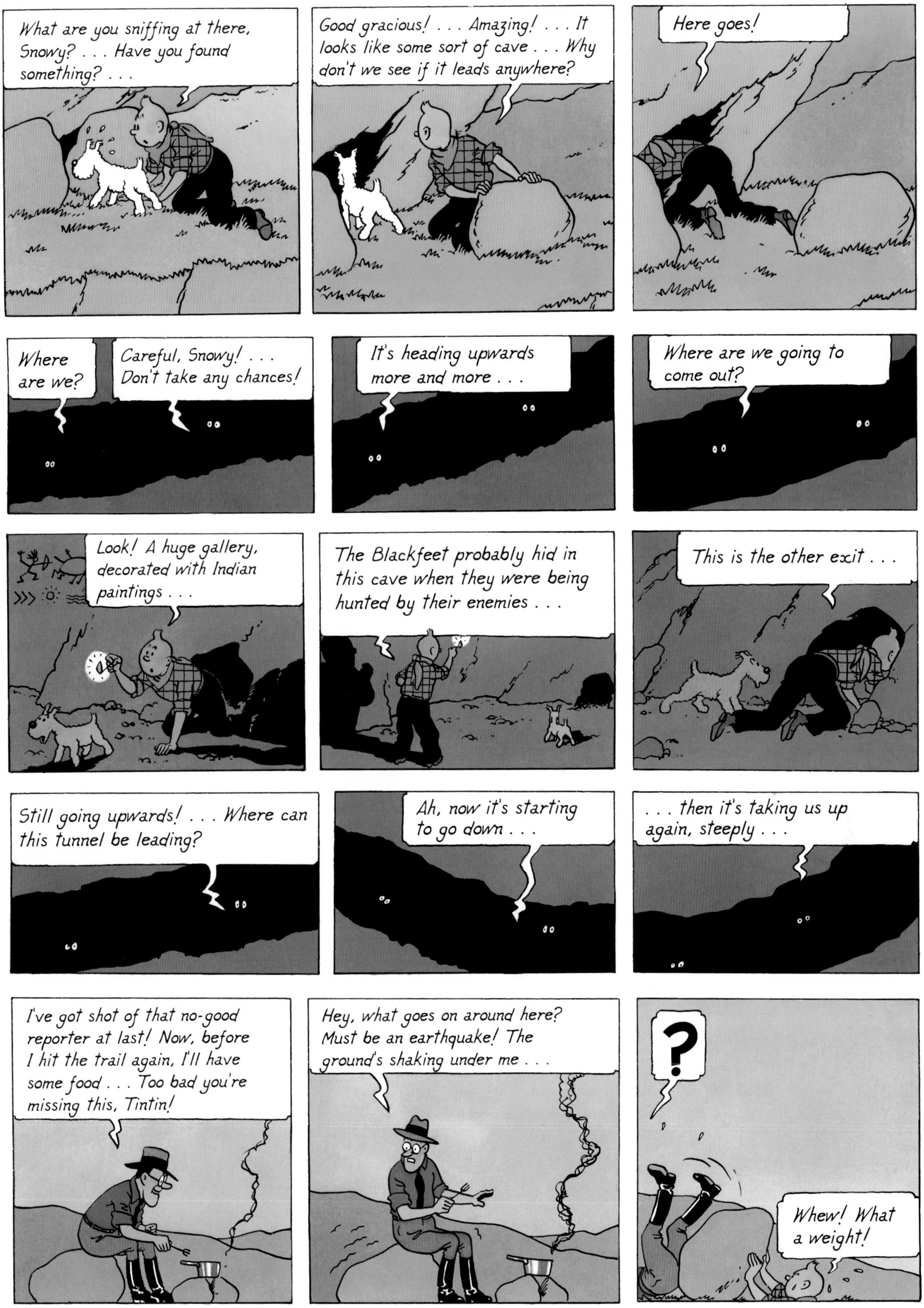

What are you sniffing at there, Snowy? . . . Have you found something? . . .
Good gracious! . . . Amazing! . . . It looks like some sort of cave . . . Why don't we see if it leads anywhere?
Here goes!
Where are we?
Careful, Snowy! . . . Don't take any chances!
It's heading upwards more and more . . .
Where are we going to come out?
Look! A huge gallery, decorated with Indian paintings . . .
The Blackfeet probably hid in this cave when they were being hunted by their enemies . . .
This is the other exit . . .
Still going upwards! . . . Where can this tunnel be leading?
Ah, now it's starting to go down . . .
. . . then it's taking us up again, steeply . . .
I've got shot of that no-good reporter at last! Now, before I hit the trail again, I'll have some food . . . Too bad you're missing this, Tintin!
Hey, what goes on around here? Must be an earthquake! The ground's shaking under me . . .
?
Whew! What a weight!

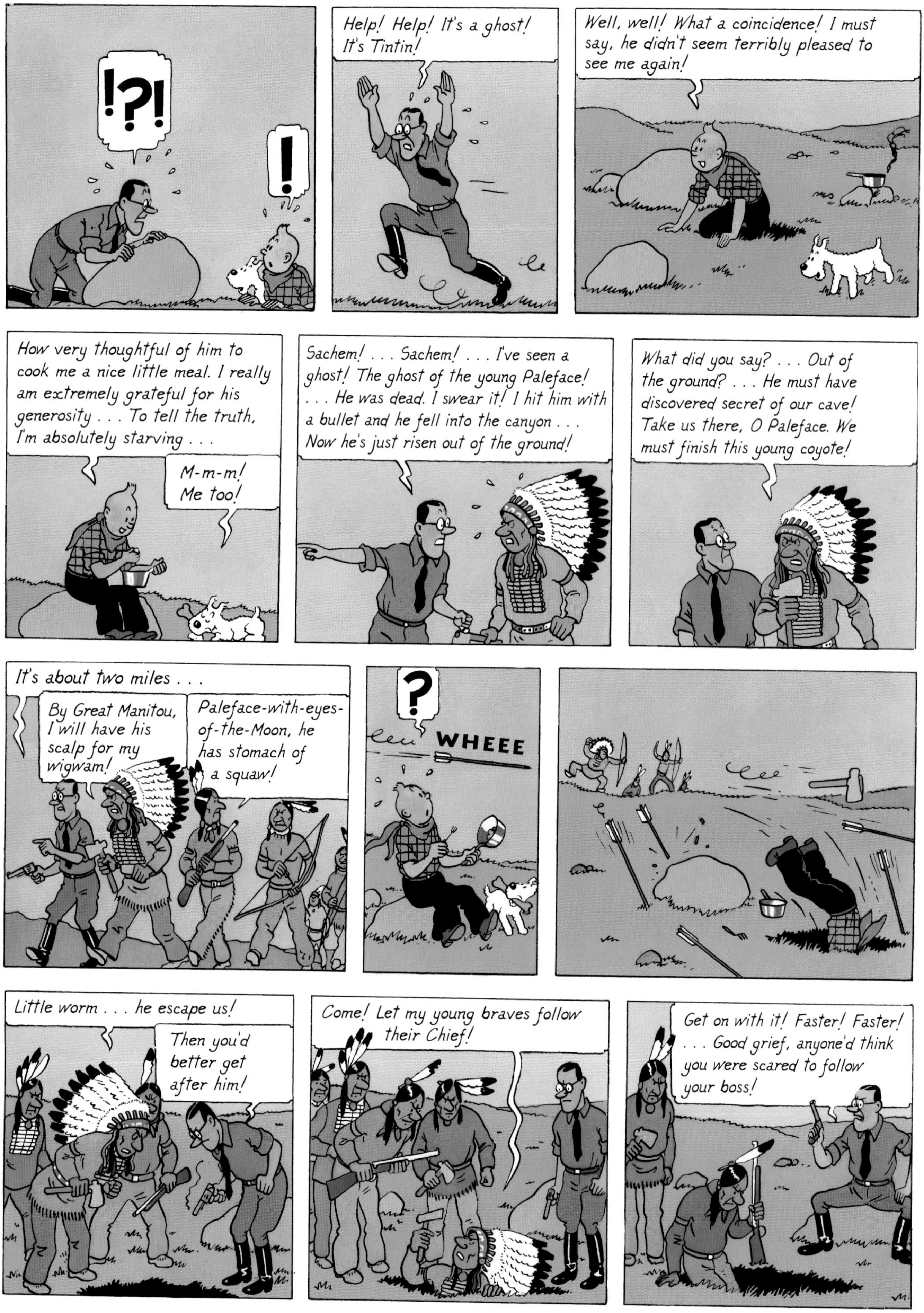

!?!
!
Help! Help! It's a ghost! It's Tintin!
Well, well! What a coincidence! I must say, he didn't seem terribly pleased to see me again!
How very thoughtful of him to cook me a nice little meal. I really am extremely grateful for his generosity . . . To tell the truth, I'm absolutely starving . . .
M-m-m! Me too!
Sachem! . . . Sachem! . . . I've seen a ghost! The ghost of the young Paleface! . . . He was dead. I swear it! I hit him with a bullet and he fell into the canyon . . . Now he's just risen out of the ground!
What did you say? . . . Out of the ground? . . . He must have discovered secret of our cave! Take us there, O Paleface. We must finish this young coyote!
It's about two miles . . .
By Great Manitou, I will have his scalp for my wigwam!
Paleface-with-eyes-of-the-Moon, he has stomach of a squaw!
?
WHEEE
Little worm . . . he escape us!
Then you'd better get after him!
Come! Let my young braves follow their Chief!
Get on with it! Faster! Faster! . . . Good grief, anyone'd think you were scared to follow your boss!

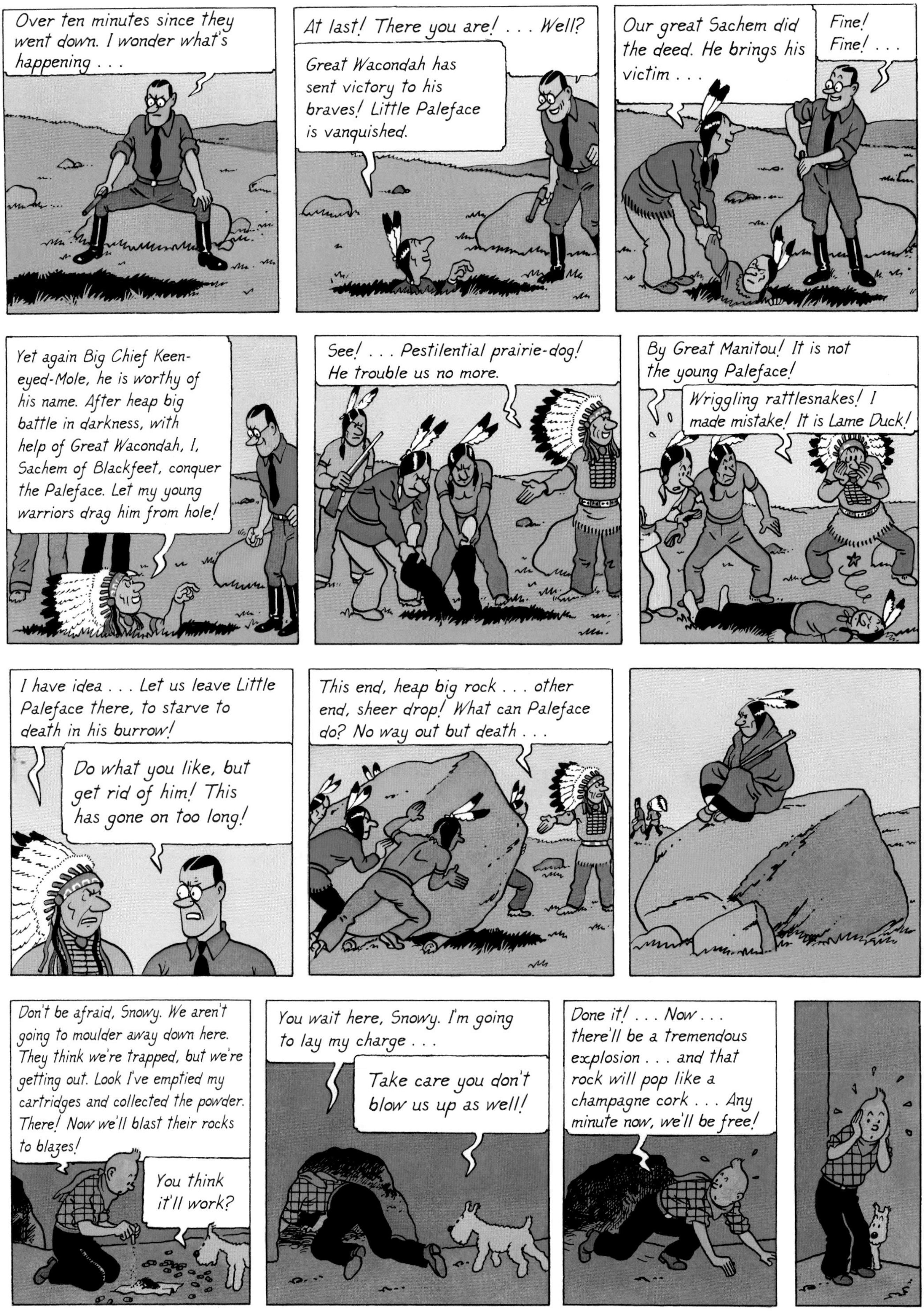

Over ten minutes since they went down. I wonder what's happening . . .
At last! There you are! . . . Well?
Great Wacondah has sent victory to his braves! Little Paleface is vanquished.
Our great Sachem did the deed. He brings his victim . . .
Fine! Fine! . . .
Yet again Big Chief Keen-eyed-Mole, he is worthy of his name. After heap big battle in darkness, with help of Great Wacondah, I, Sachem of Blackfeet, conquer the Paleface. Let my young warriors drag him from hole!
See! . . . Pestilential prairie-dog! He trouble us no more.
By Great Manitou! It is not the young Paleface!
Wriggling rattlesnakes! I made mistake! It is Lame Duck!
I have idea . . . Let us leave Little Paleface there, to starve to death in his burrow!
Do what you like, but get rid of him! This has gone on too long!
This end, heap big rock . . . other end, sheer drop! What can Paleface do? No way out but death . . .
Don't be afraid, Snowy. We aren't going to moulder away down here. They think we're trapped, but we're getting out. Look I've emptied my cartridges and collected the powder. There! Now we'll blast their rocks to blazes!
You think it'll work?
You wait here, Snowy. I'm going to lay my charge . . .
Take care you don't blow us up as well!
Done it! . . . Now . . . there'll be a tremendous explosion . . . and that rock will pop like a champagne cork . . . Any minute now, we'll be free!

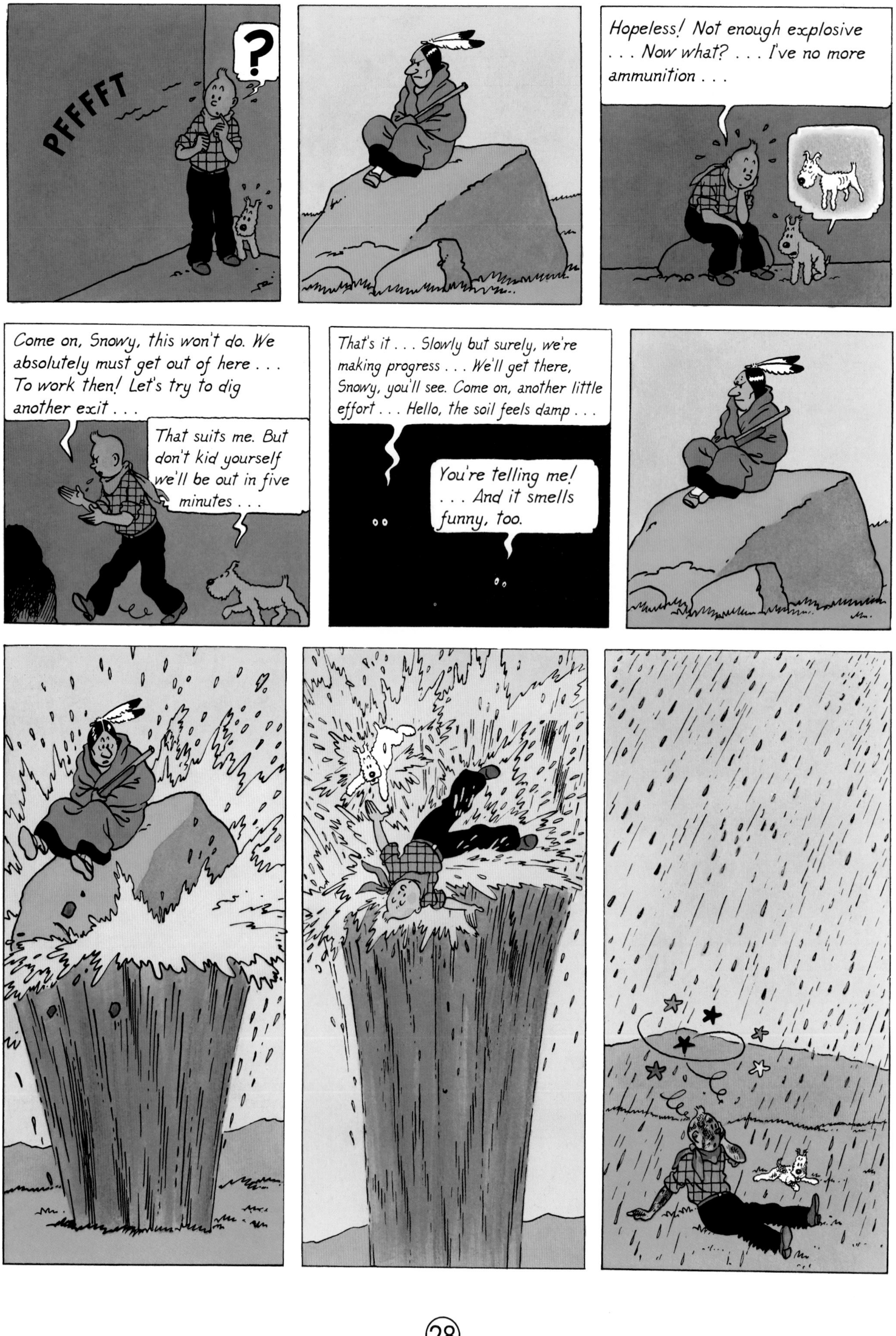
PFFFFT
?
Hopeless! Not enough explosive . . . Now what? . . . I've no more ammunition . . .
Come on, Snowy, this won't do. We absolutely must get out of here . . . To work then! Let's try to dig another exit . . .
That suits me. But don't kid yourself we'll be out in five minutes . . .
That's it . . . Slowly but surely, we're making progress . . . We'll get there, Snowy, you'll see. Come on, another little effort . . . Hello, the soil feels damp . . .
You're telling me! . . . And it smells funny, too.

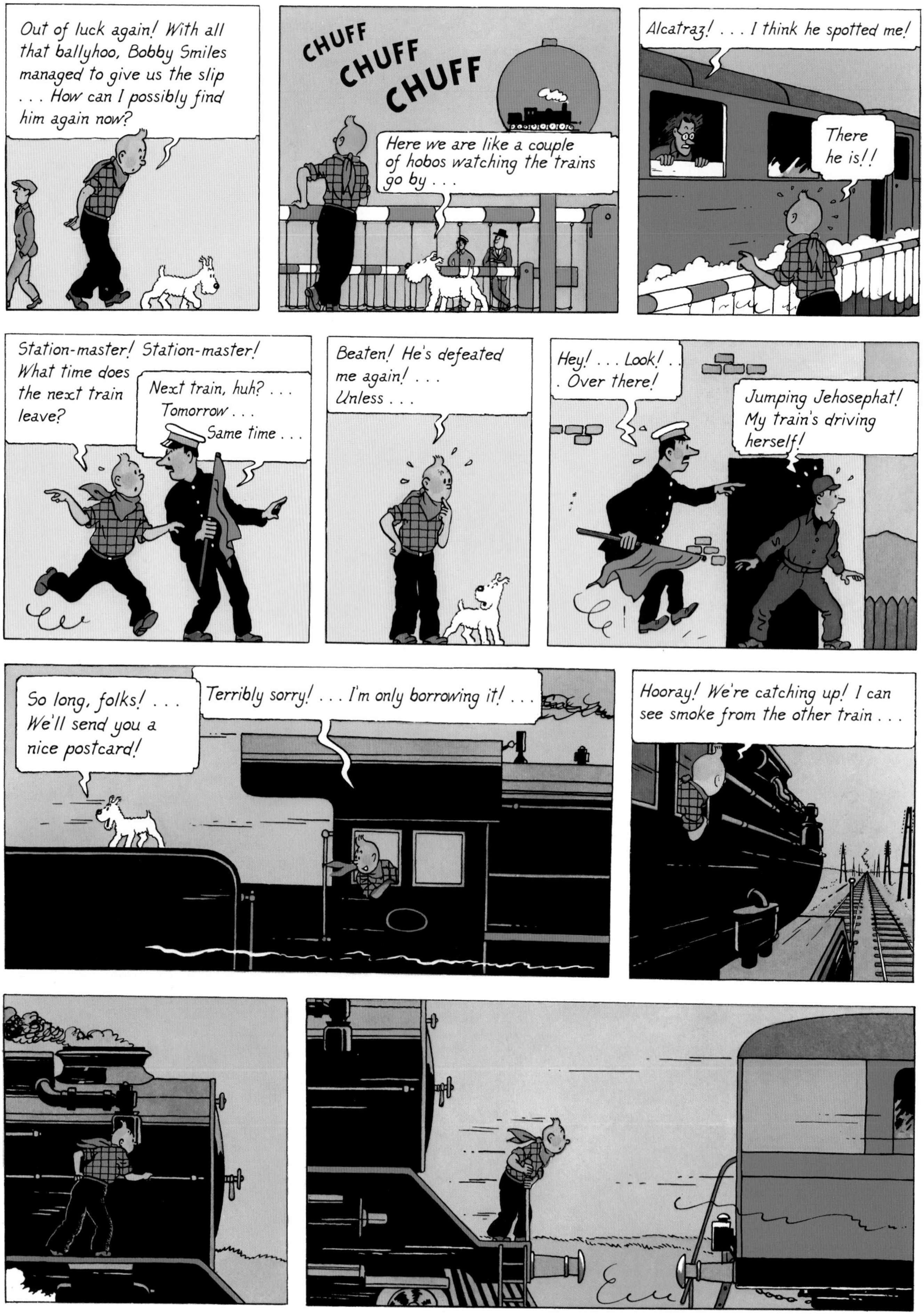
Out of luck again! With all that ballyhoo, Bobby Smiles managed to give us the slip . . . How can I possibly find him again now?
CHUFF CHUFF CHUFF
Here we are like a couple of hobos watching the trains go by . . .
Alcatraz! . . . I think he spotted me!
There he is!!
Station-master! Station-master! What time does the next train leave?
Next train, huh? . . . Tomorrow . . . Same time . . .
Beaten! He's defeated me again! . . . Unless . . .
Hey! . . . Look! . . . Over there!
Jumping Jehosephat! My train's driving herself!
So long, folks! . . . We'll send you a nice postcard!
Terribly sorry! . . . I'm only borrowing it! . . .
Hooray! We're catching up! I can see smoke from the other train . . .

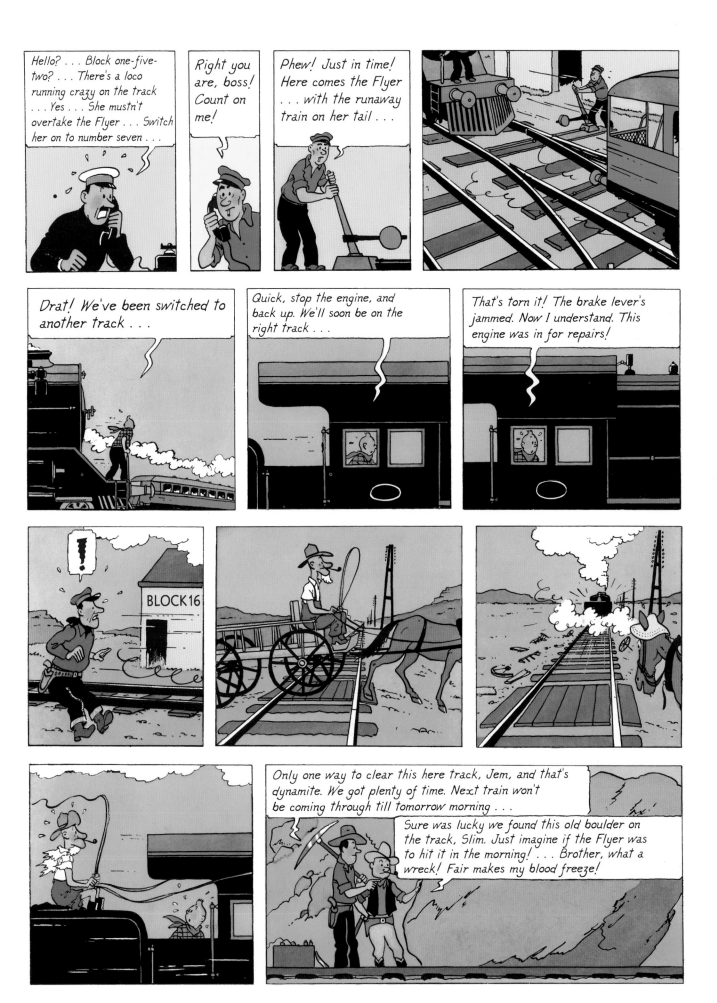

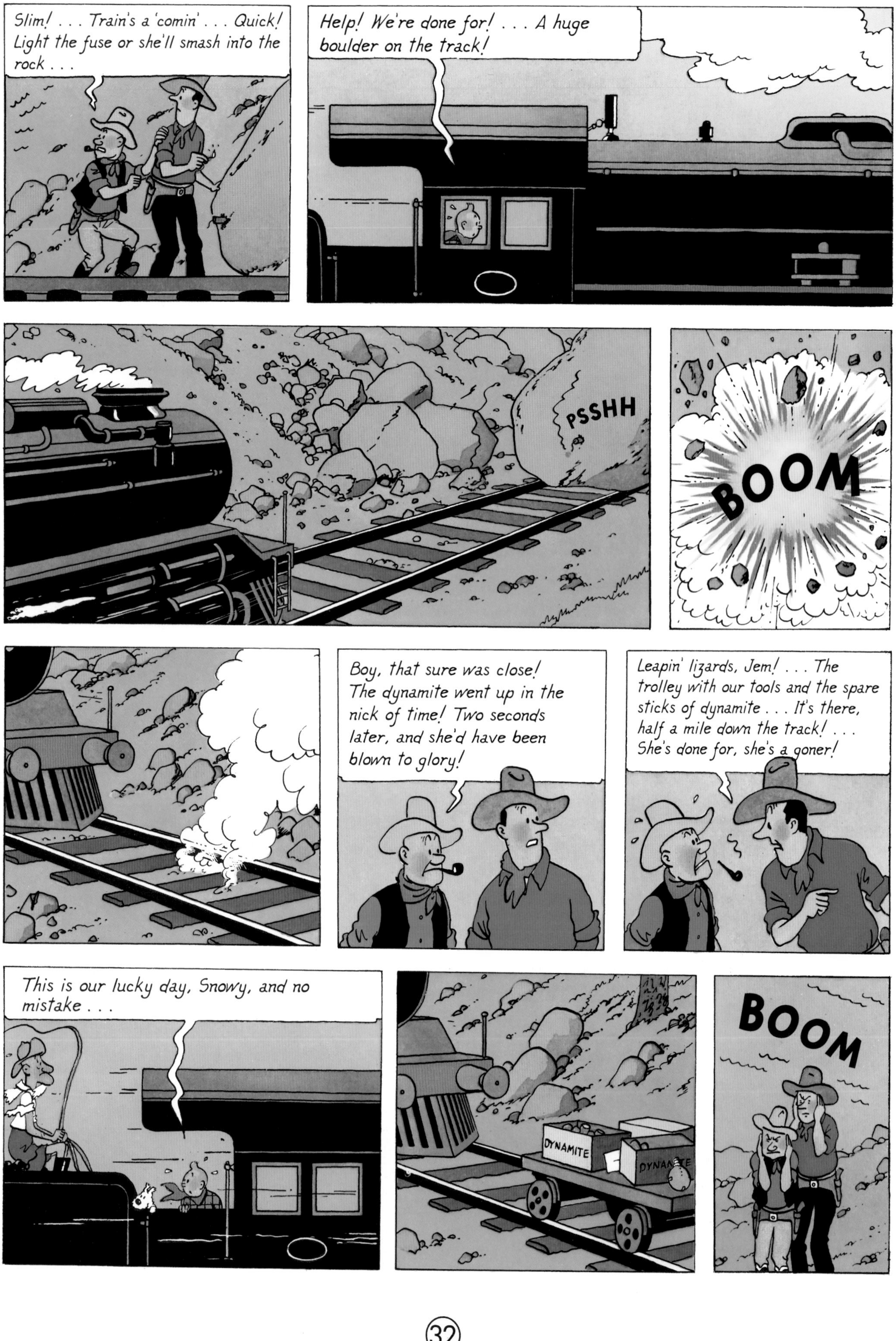
Slim! . . . Train's a 'comin' . . . Quick! Light the fuse or she'll smash into the rock . . .
Help! We're done for! . . . A huge boulder on the track!
PSSHH
BOOM
Boy, that sure was close! The dynamite went up in the nick of time! Two seconds later, and she'd have been blown to glory!
Leapin' lizards, Jem! . . . The trolley with our tools and the spare sticks of dynamite . . . It's there, half a mile down the track! . . . She's done for, she's a goner!
This is our lucky day, Snowy, and no mistake . . .
DYNAMITE
BOOM

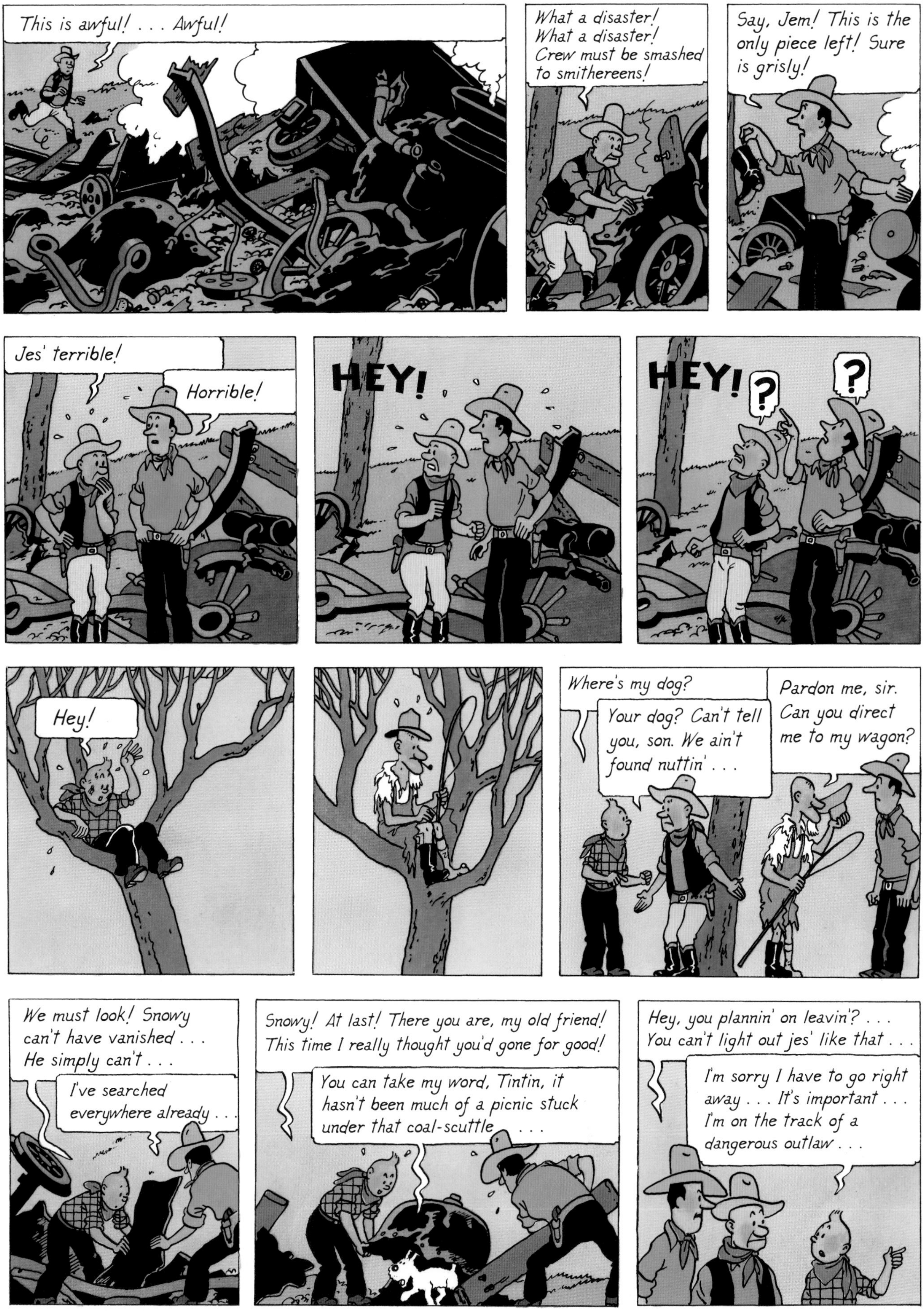
This is awful! . . . Awful!
What a disaster! What a disaster! Crew must be smashed to smithereens!
Say, Jem! This is the only piece left! Sure is grisly!
Jes' terrible!
Horrible!
HEY!
HEY!
?
?
Hey!
Where's my dog?
Your dog? Can't tell you, son. We ain't found nuttin' . . .
Pardon me, sir. Can you direct me to my wagon?
We must look! Snowy can't have vanished . . . He simply can't . . .
I've searched everywhere already . . .
Snowy! At last! There you are, my old friend! This time I really thought you'd gone for good!
You can take my word, Tintin, it hasn't been much of a picnic stuck under that coal-scuttle . . .
Hey, you plannin' on leavin'? . . . You can't light out jes' like that . . .
I'm sorry I have to go right away . . . It's important . . . I'm on the track of a dangerous outlaw . . .

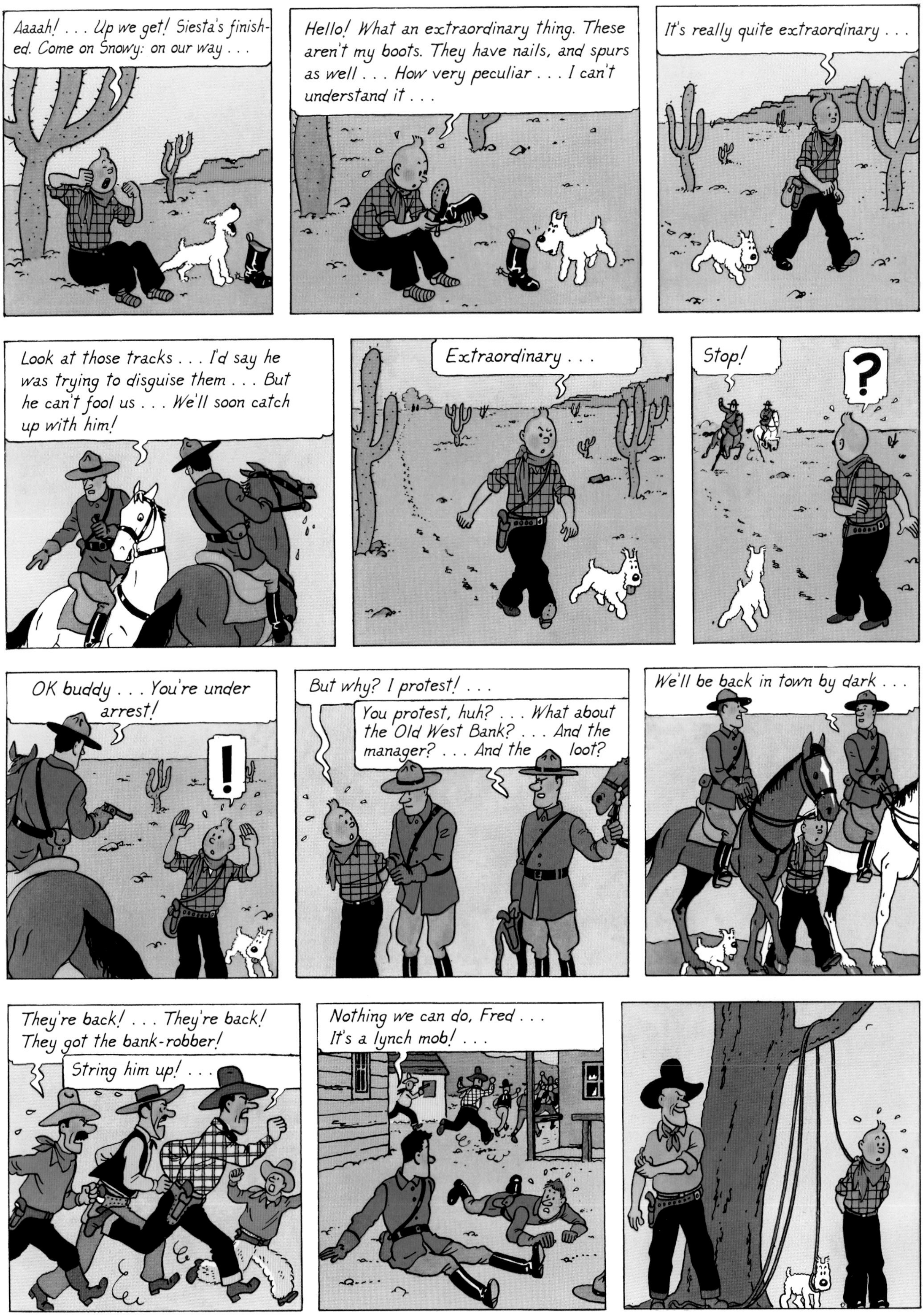
Aaaah! . . . Up we get! Siesta's finish-ed. Come on Snowy: on our way . . .
Hello! What an extraordinary thing. These aren't my boots. They have nails, and spurs as well . . . How very peculiar . . . I can't understand it . . .
It's really quite extraordinary . . .
Look at those tracks . . . I'd say he was trying to disguise them . . . But he can't fool us . . . We'll soon catch up with him!
Extraordinary . . .
Stop!
?
OK buddy . . . You're under arrest!
!
But why? I protest! . . .
You protest, huh? . . . What about the Old West Bank? . . . And the manager? . . . And the loot?
We'll be back in town by dark . . .
They're back! . . . They're back! They got the bank-robber!
String him up! . . .
Nothing we can do, Fred . . . It's a lynch mob! . . .

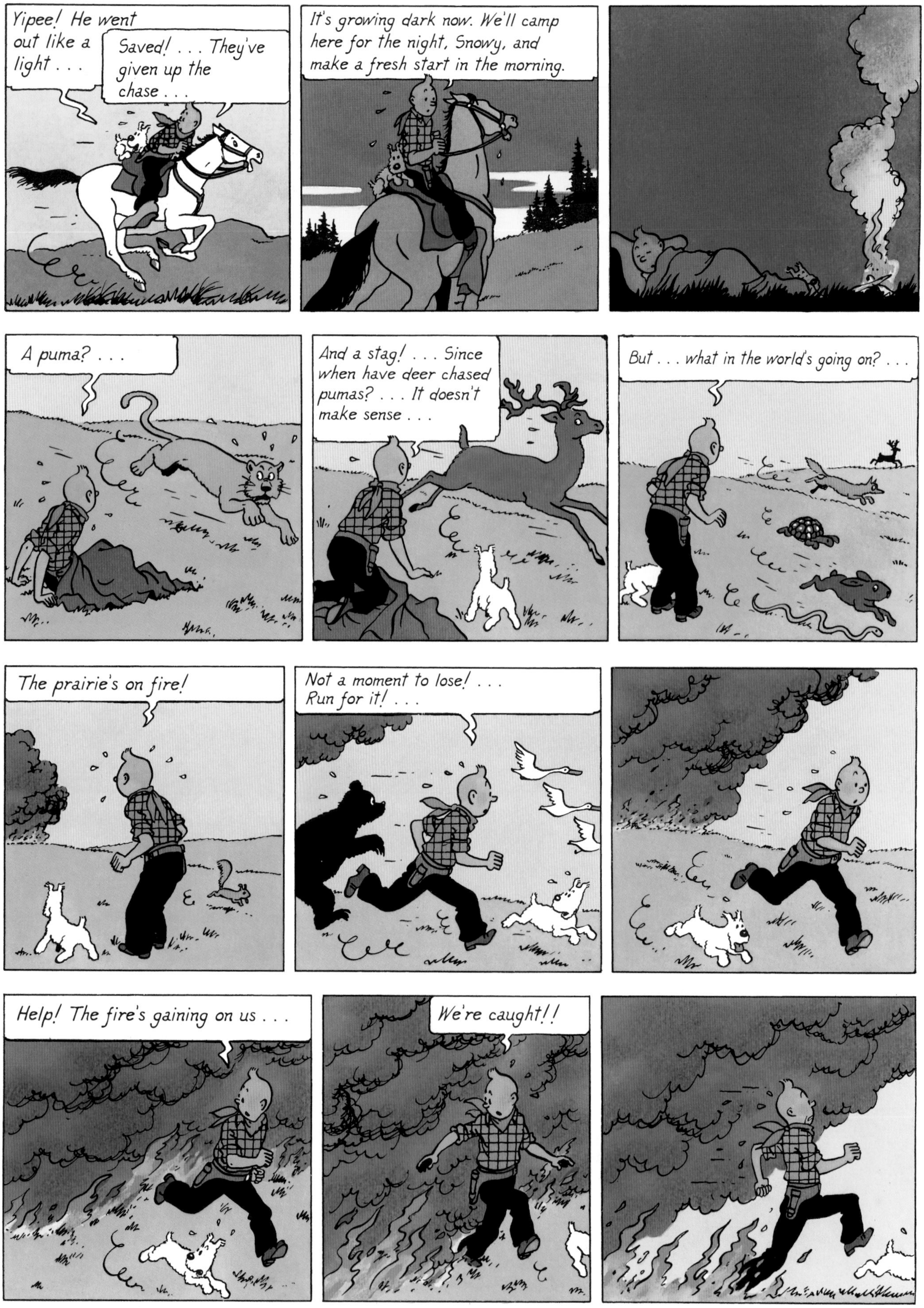
Yipee! He went out like a light . . .
Saved! . . . They've given up the chase . . .
It's growing dark now. We'll camp here for the night, Snowy, and make a fresh start in the morning.
A puma? . . .
And a stag! . . . Since when have deer chased pumas? . . . It doesn't make sense . . .
But . . . what in the world's going on? . . .
The prairie's on fire!
Not a moment to lose! . . . Run for it! . . .
Help! The fire's gaining on us . . .
We're caught!!

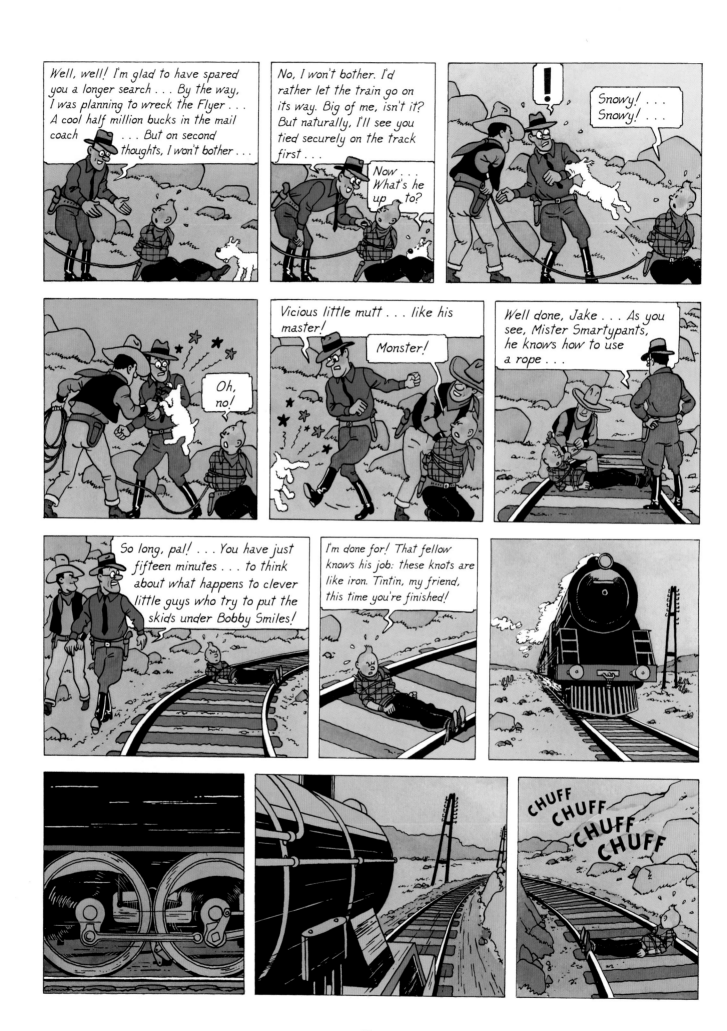

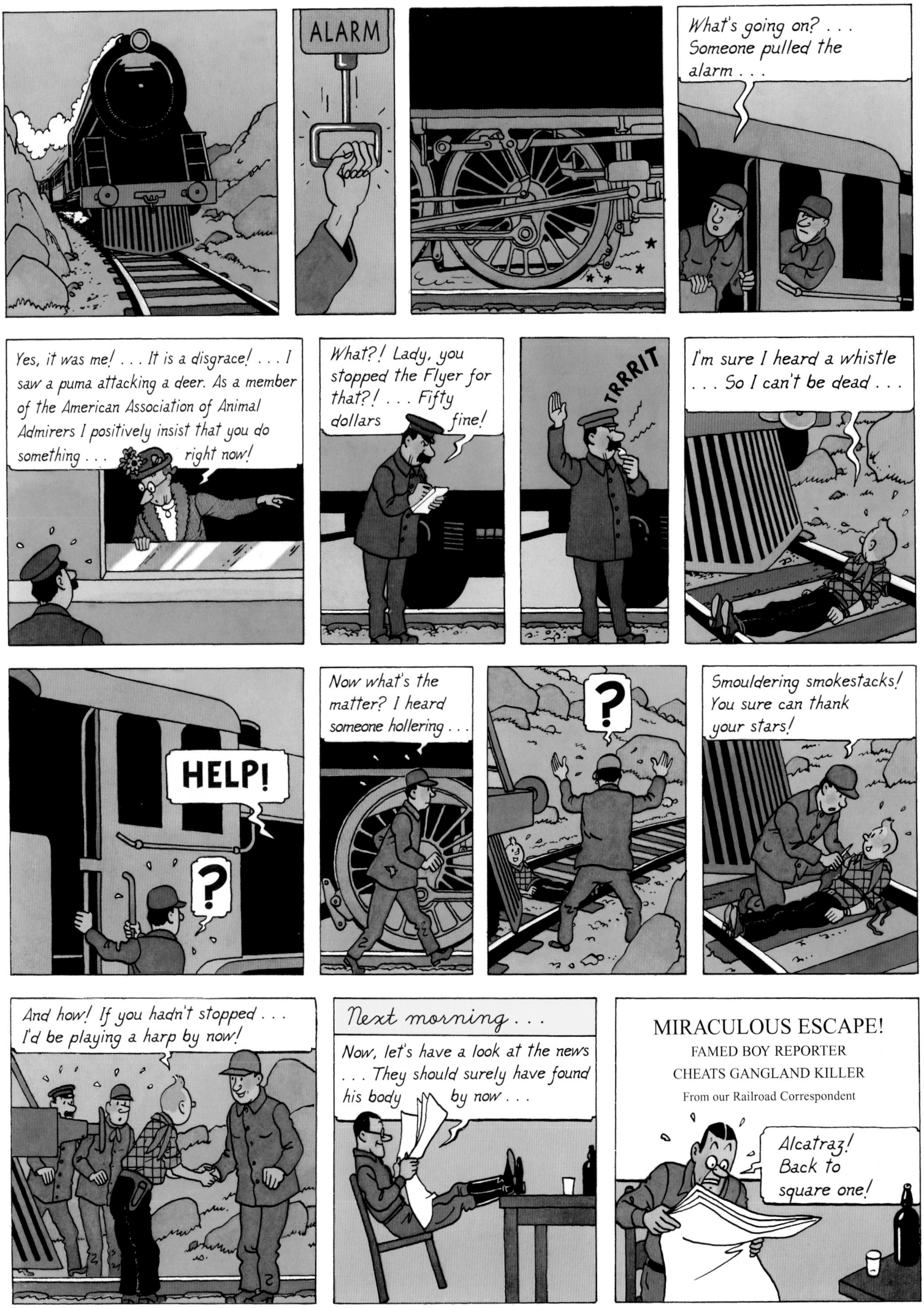
ALARM
What's going on? . . . Someone pulled the alarm . . .
Yes, it was me! . . . It is a disgrace! . . . I saw a puma attacking a deer. As a member of the American Association of Animal Admirers I positively insist that you do something . . . right now!
What?! Lady, you stopped the Flyer for that?! . . . Fifty dollars fine!
TRRRIT
I'm sure I heard a whistle . . . So I can't be dead . . .
HELP!
?
Now what's the matter? I heard someone hollering . . .
?
Smouldering smokestacks! You sure can thank your stars!
And how! If you hadn't stopped . . . I'd be playing a harp by now!
Next morning . . .
Now, let's have a look at the news . . . They should surely have found his body by now . . .
MIRACULOUS ESCAPE!
FAMED BOY REPORTER
CHEATS GANGLAND KILLER
From our Railroad Correspondent
Alcatraz! Back to square one!

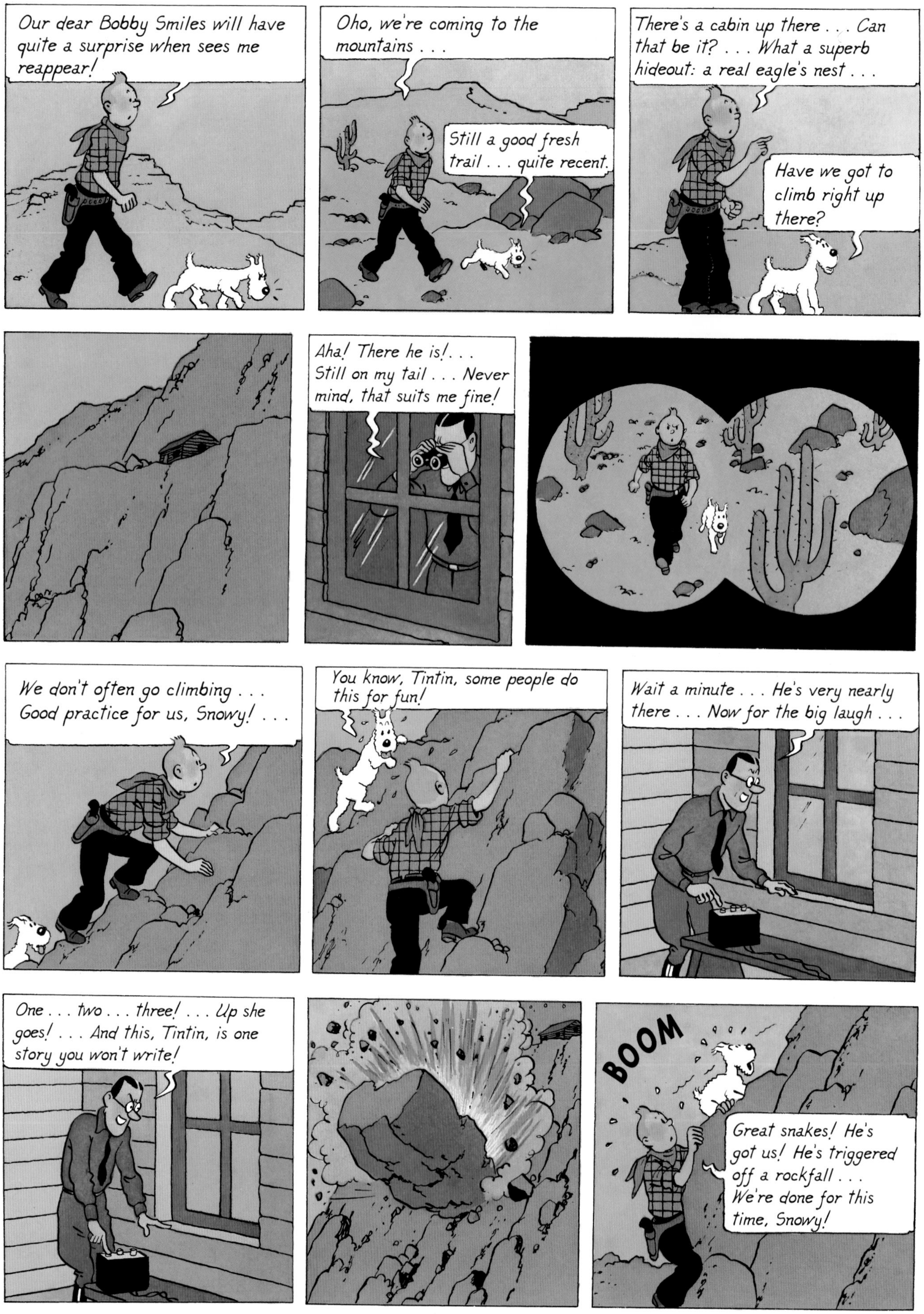
Our dear Bobby Smiles will have quite a surprise when sees me reappear!
Oho, we're coming to the mountains . . .
Still a good fresh trail . . . quite recent.
There's a cabin up there . . . Can that be it? . . . What a superb hideout: a real eagle's nest . . .
Have we got to climb right up there?
Aha! There he is! . . . Still on my tail . . . Never mind, that suits me fine!
We don't often go climbing . . . Good practice for us, Snowy! . . .
You know, Tintin, some people do this for fun!
Wait a minute . . . He's very nearly there . . . Now for the big laugh . . .
One . . . two . . . three! . . . Up she goes! . . . And this, Tintin, is one story you won't write!
BOOM
Great snakes! He's got us! He's triggered off a rockfall . . . We're done for this time, Snowy!

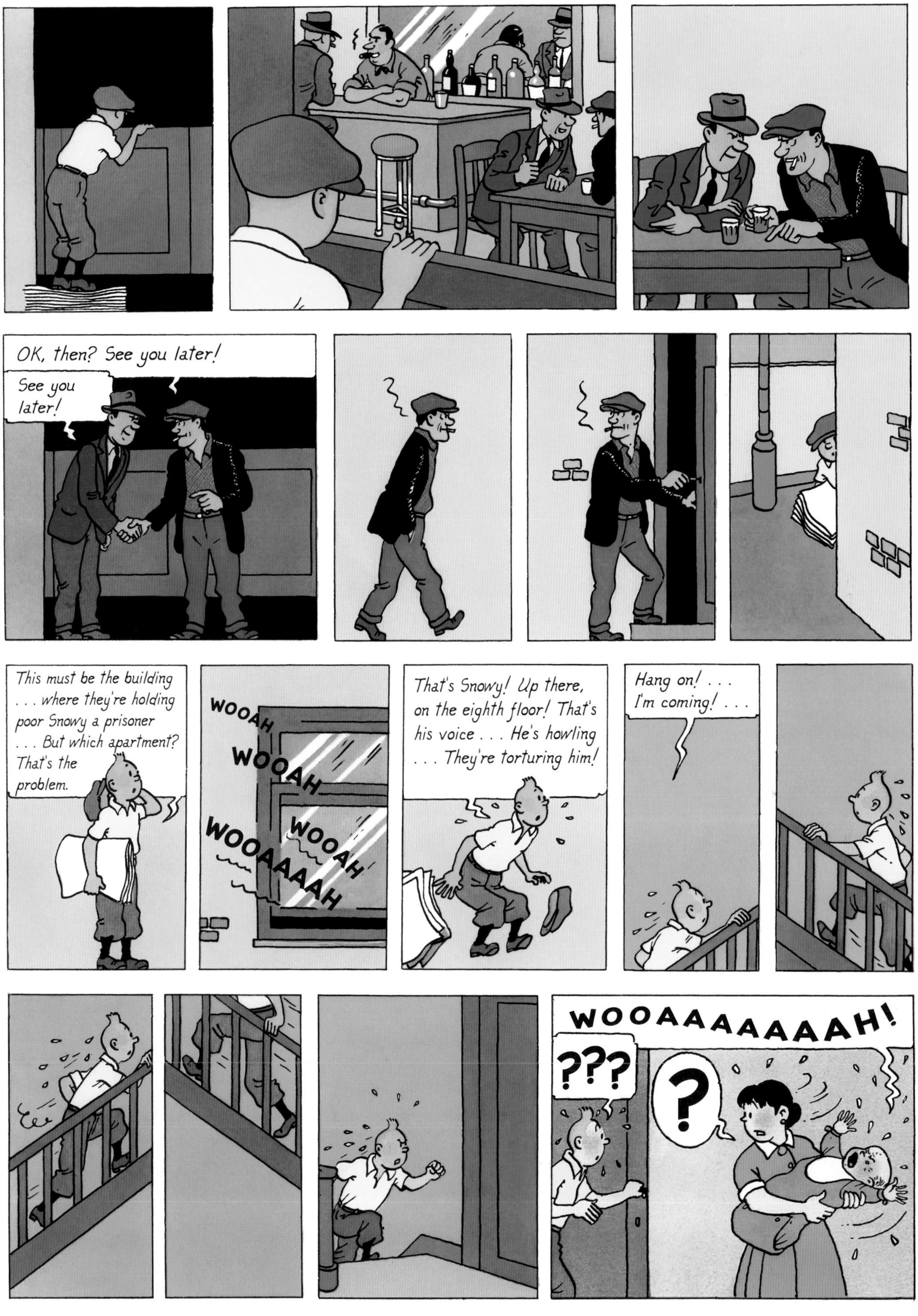

OK, then? See you later!
See you later!
This must be the building . . . where they're holding poor Snowy a prisoner . . . But which apartment? That's the problem.
WOOAH
WOOAH
WOOAH
WOOAAAAAH
That's Snowy! Up there, on the eighth floor! That's his voice . . . He's howling . . . They're torturing him!
Hang on! . . . I'm coming! . . .
WOOAAAAAAAAH!
???
?

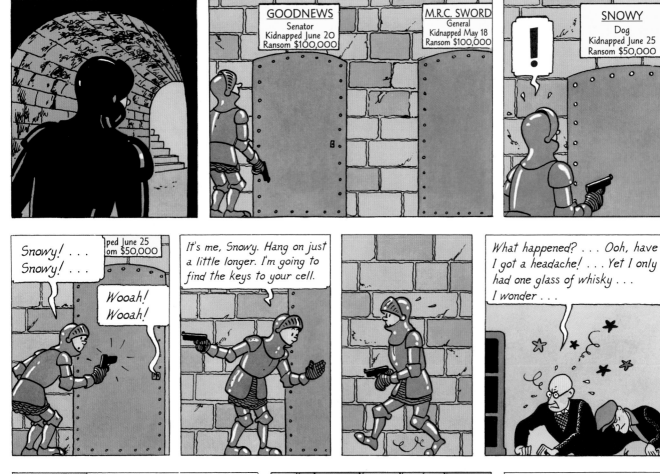

GOODNEWS
Senator
Kidnapped June 20
Ransom $100,000

M.R.C. SWORD
General
Kidnapped May 18
Ransom $100,000

!

SNOWY
Dog
Kidnapped June 25
Ransom $50,000

Snowy! . . .
Snowy! . . .

ped June 25
om $50,000

Wooah!
Wooah!

It's me, Snowy. Hang on just a little longer. I'm going to find the keys to your cell.

What happened? . . . Ooh, have I got a headache! . . . Yet I only had one glass of whisky . . . I wonder . . .

Hey! . . . Just you keep quiet for a bit!

Here I am, Snowy! You see, Tintin hasn't let you down!

Snowy! My dear old Snowy!

I never thought . . . I'd ever see you again . . .

KIDNAP INC.
RULES FOR GUESTS

Ssh! A whistle! . . . One of the gangsters upstairs must have raised the alarm . . . We'd better watch out . . .

That's a snappy outfit Tintin . . .

He's around here somewhere. I give you ten minutes . . . Bring him to me . . . bound and gagged. Now, get going . . . Scram!

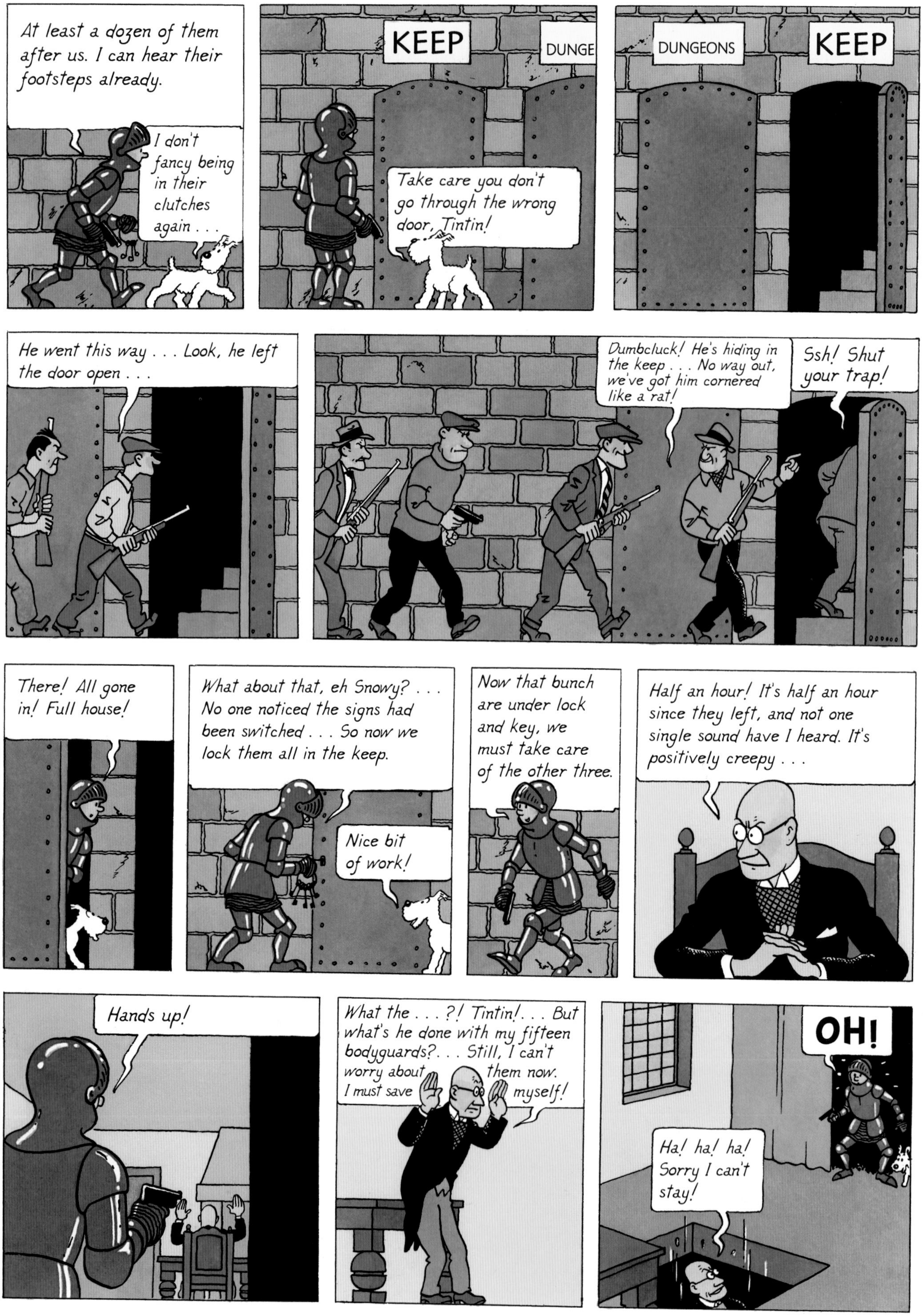
At least a dozen of them after us. I can hear their footsteps already.
I don't fancy being in their clutches again . . .
KEEP
DUNGE
Take care you don't go through the wrong door, Tintin!
DUNGEONS
KEEP
He went this way . . . Look, he left the door open . . .
Dumbcluck! He's hiding in the keep . . . No way out, we've got him cornered like a rat!
Ssh! Shut your trap!
There! All gone in! Full house!
What about that, eh Snowy? . . . No one noticed the signs had been switched . . . So now we lock them all in the keep.
Nice bit of work!
Now that bunch are under lock and key, we must take care of the other three.
Half an hour! It's half an hour since they left, and not one single sound have I heard. It's positively creepy . . .
Hands up!
What the . . . ?! Tintin! . . . But what's he done with my fifteen bodyguards? . . . Still, I can't worry about them now. I must save myself!
OH!
Ha! ha! ha! Sorry I can't stay!

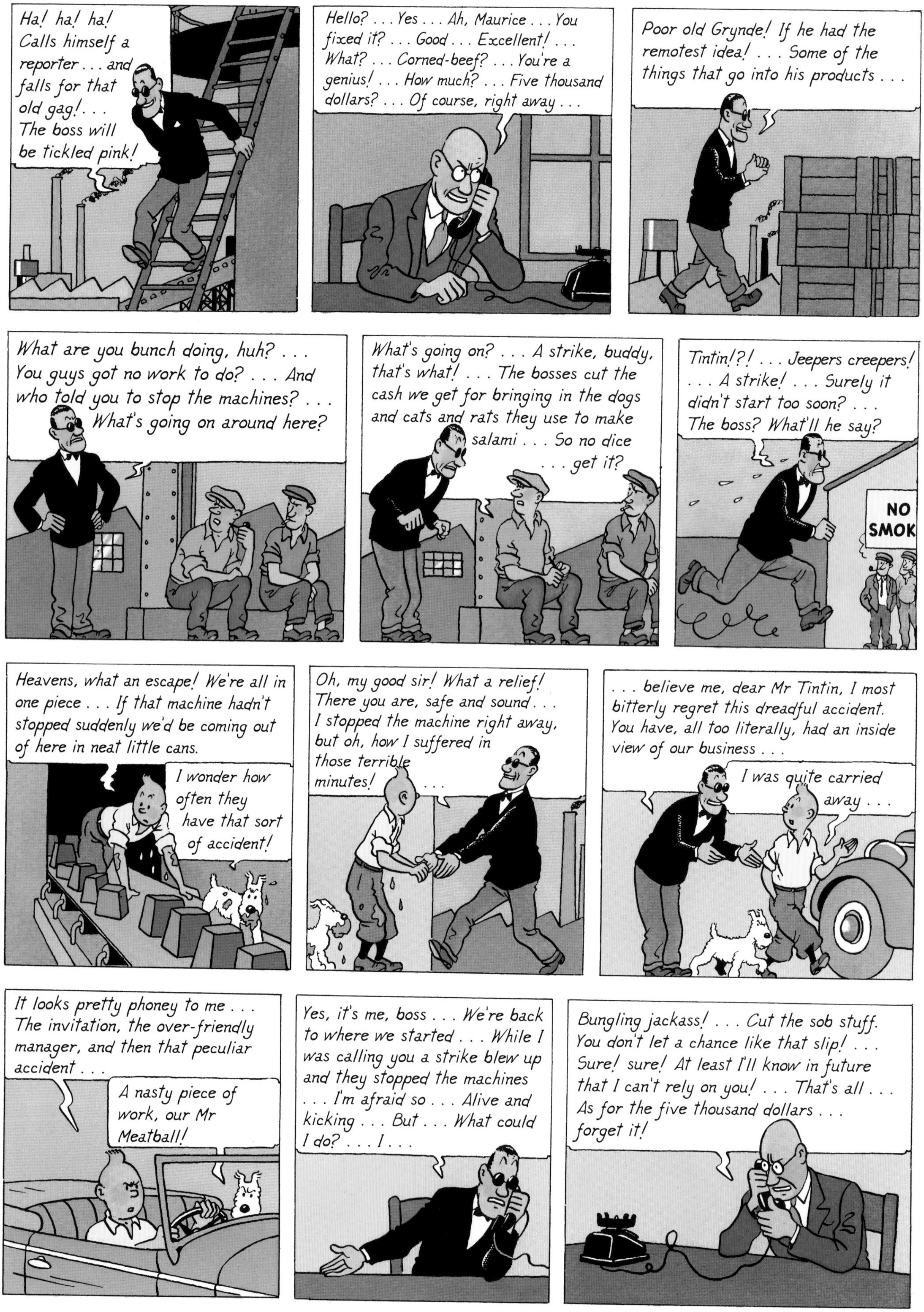

Ha! ha! ha! Calls himself a reporter . . . and falls for that old gag! . . . The boss will be tickled pink!
Hello? . . . Yes . . . Ah, Maurice . . . You fixed it? . . . Good . . . Excellent! . . . What? . . . Corned-beef? . . . You're a genius! . . . How much? . . . Five thousand dollars? . . . Of course, right away . . .
Poor old Grynde! If he had the remotest idea! . . . Some of the things that go into his products . . .
What are you bunch doing, huh? . . . You guys got no work to do? . . . And who told you to stop the machines? . . . What's going on around here?
What's going on? . . . A strike, buddy, that's what! . . . The bosses cut the cash we get for bringing in the dogs and cats and rats they use to make salami . . . So no dice . . . get it?
Tintin!?! . . . Jeepers creepers! . . . A strike! . . . Surely it didn't start too soon? . . . The boss? What'll he say?
NO SMOK
Heavens, what an escape! We're all in one piece . . . If that machine hadn't stopped suddenly we'd be coming out of here in neat little cans.
I wonder how often they have that sort of accident!
Oh, my good sir! What a relief! There you are, safe and sound . . . I stopped the machine right away, but oh, how I suffered in those terrible minutes! . . .
. . . believe me, dear Mr Tintin, I most bitterly regret this dreadful accident. You have, all too literally, had an inside view of our business . . .
I was quite carried away . . .
It looks pretty phoney to me . . . The invitation, the over-friendly manager, and then that peculiar accident . . .
A nasty piece of work, our Mr Meatball!
Yes, it's me, boss . . . We're back to where we started . . . While I was calling you a strike blew up and they stopped the machines . . . I'm afraid so . . . Alive and kicking . . . But . . . What could I do? . . . I . . .
Bungling jackass! . . . Cut the sob stuff. You don't let a chance like that slip! . . . Sure! sure! At least I'll know in future that I can't rely on you! . . . That's all . . . As for the five thousand dollars . . . forget it!

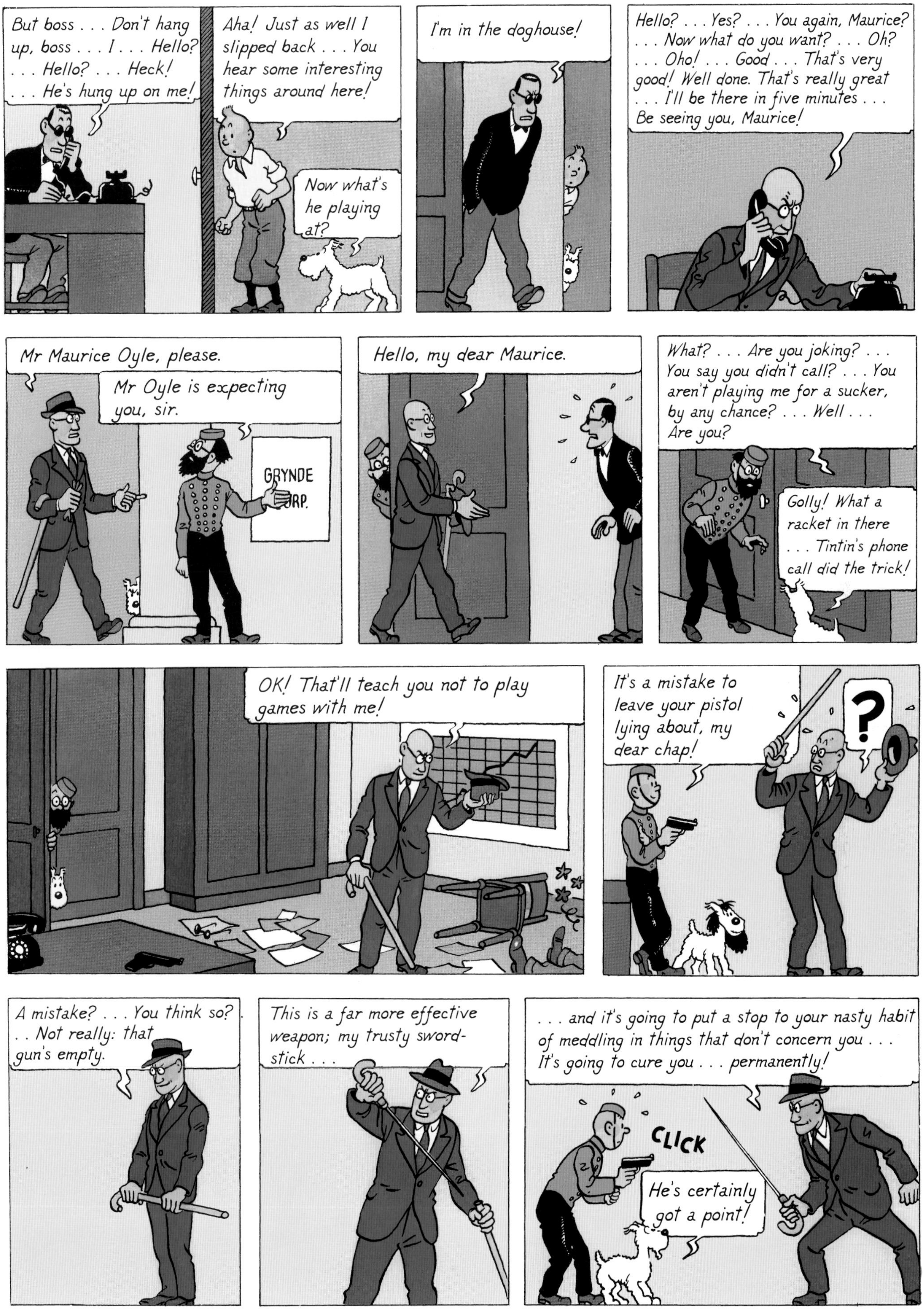
But boss . . . Don't hang up, boss . . . I . . . Hello? . . . Hello? . . . Heck! . . . He's hung up on me!
Aha! Just as well I slipped back . . . You hear some interesting things around here!
Now what's he playing at?
I'm in the doghouse!
Hello? . . . Yes? . . . You again, Maurice? . . . Now what do you want? . . . Oh? . . . Oho! . . . Good . . . That's very good! Well done. That's really great . . . I'll be there in five minutes . . . Be seeing you, Maurice!
Mr Maurice Oyle, please.
Mr Oyle is expecting you, sir.
GRYNDE
RP.
Hello, my dear Maurice.
What? . . . Are you joking? . . . You say you didn't call? . . . You aren't playing me for a sucker, by any chance? . . . Well . . . Are you?
Golly! What a racket in there . . . Tintin's phone call did the trick!
OK! That'll teach you not to play games with me!
It's a mistake to leave your pistol lying about, my dear chap!
?
A mistake? . . . You think so? . . . Not really: that gun's empty.
This is a far more effective weapon; my trusty sword-stick . . .
. . . and it's going to put a stop to your nasty habit of meddling in things that don't concern you . . . It's going to cure you . . . permanently!
CLICK
He's certainly got a point!

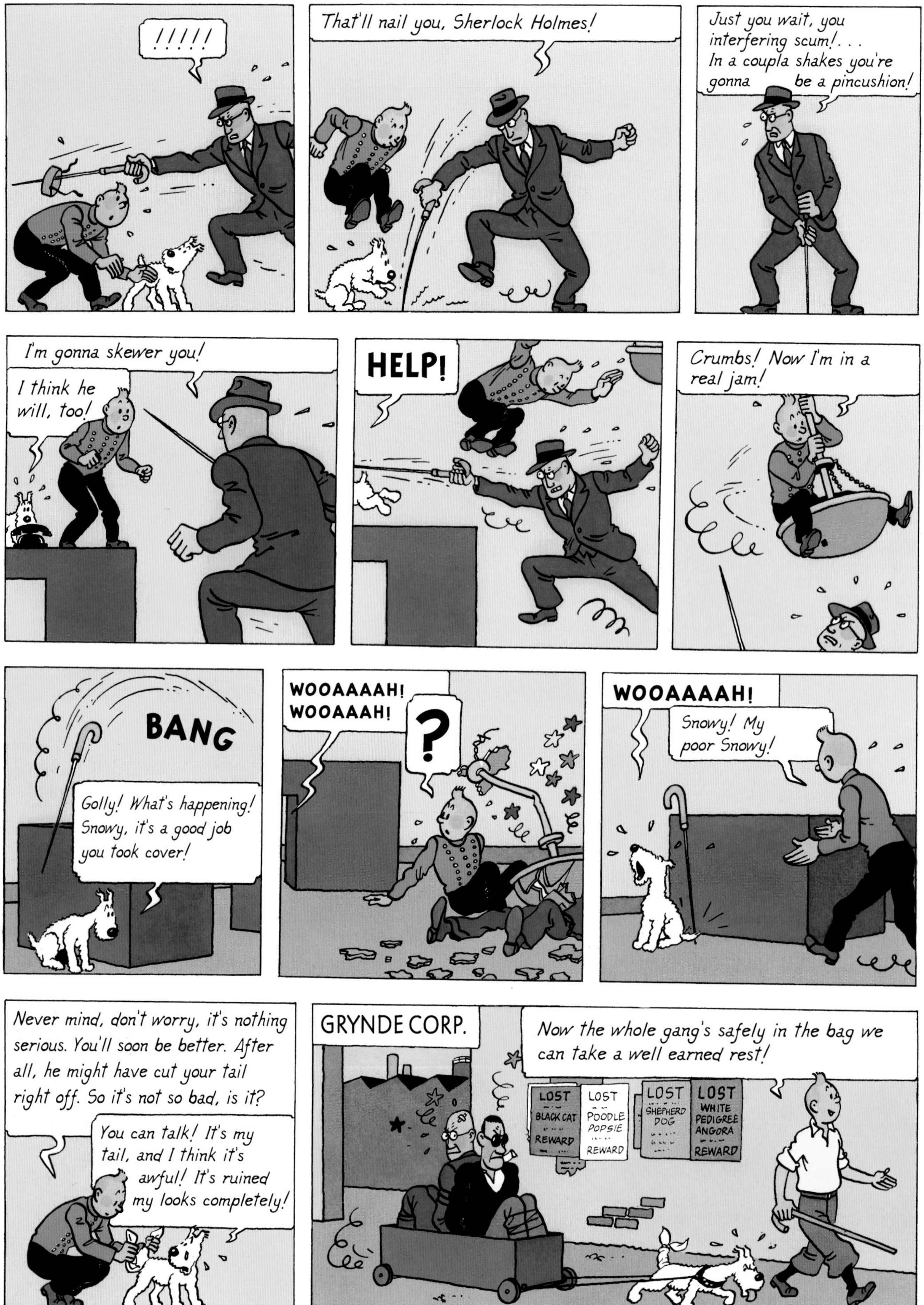
!!!!!
That'll nail you, Sherlock Holmes!
Just you wait, you interfering scum!. . . In a coupla shakes you're gonna be a pincushion!
I'm gonna skewer you!
I think he will, too!
HELP!
Crumbs! Now I'm in a real jam!
BANG
Golly! What's happening! Snowy, it's a good job you took cover!
WOOAAAAH! WOOAAAH!
?
WOOAAAAH!
Snowy! My poor Snowy!
Never mind, don't worry, it's nothing serious. You'll soon be better. After all, he might have cut your tail right off. So it's not so bad, is it?
You can talk! It's my tail, and I think it's awful! It's ruined my looks completely!
GRYNDE CORP.
Now the whole gang's safely in the bag we can take a well earned rest!
LOST BLACK CAT REWARD
LOST POODLE POPSIE REWARD
LOST SHEPHERD DOG
LOST WHITE PEDIGREE ANGORA REWARD

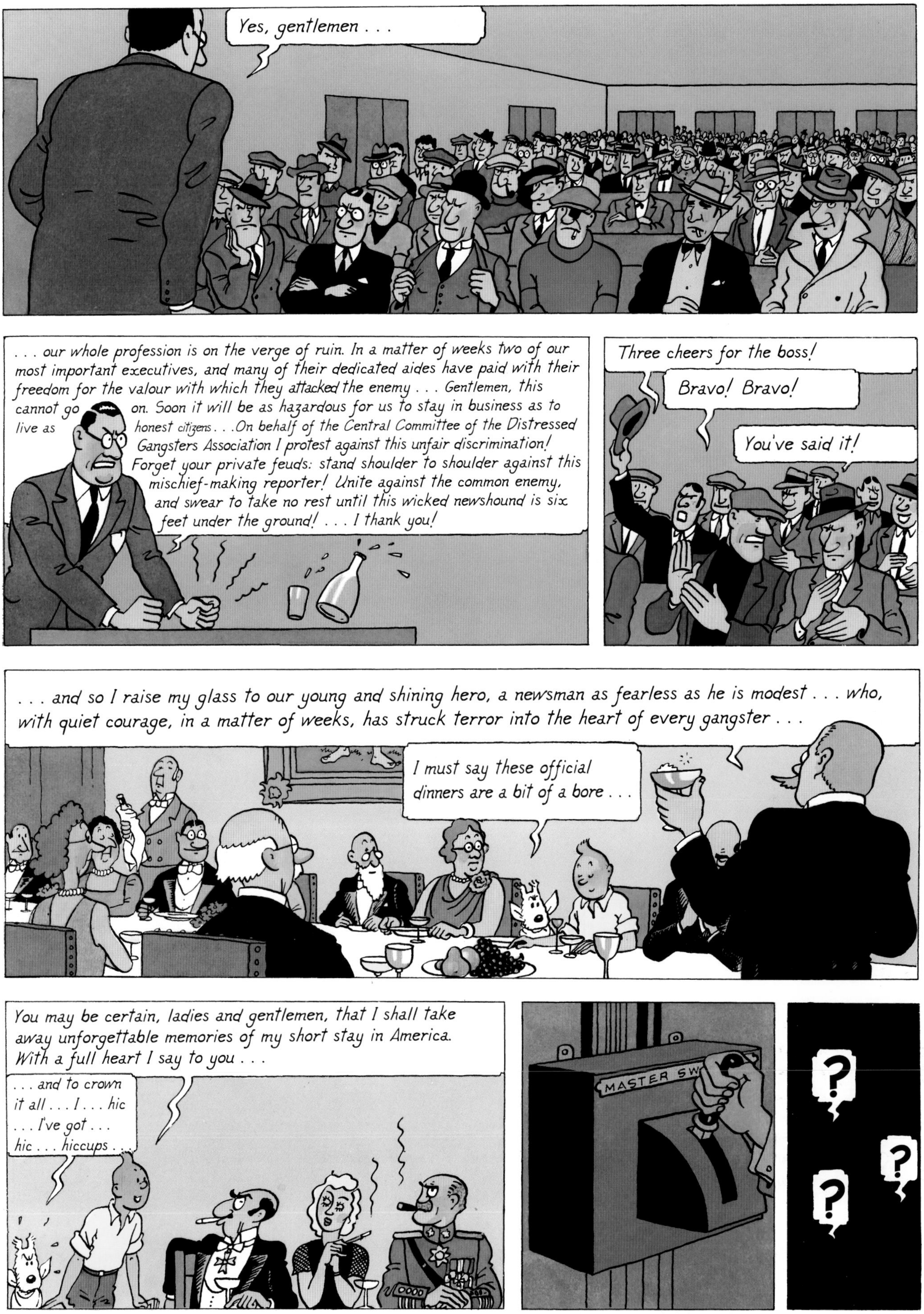
Yes, gentlemen . . .
. . . our whole profession is on the verge of ruin. In a matter of weeks two of our most important executives, and many of their dedicated aides have paid with their freedom for the valour with which they attacked the enemy . . . Gentlemen, this cannot go on. Soon it will be as hazardous for us to stay in business as to live as honest citizens . . . On behalf of the Central Committee of the Distressed Gangsters Association I protest against this unfair discrimination! Forget your private feuds: stand shoulder to shoulder against this mischief-making reporter! Unite against the common enemy, and swear to take no rest until this wicked newshound is six feet under the ground! . . . I thank you!
Three cheers for the boss!
Bravo! Bravo!
You've said it!
. . . and so I raise my glass to our young and shining hero, a newsman as fearless as he is modest . . . who, with quiet courage, in a matter of weeks, has struck terror into the heart of every gangster . . .
I must say these official dinners are a bit of a bore . . .
You may be certain, ladies and gentlemen, that I shall take away unforgettable memories of my short stay in America. With a full heart I say to you . . .
. . . and to crown it all . . . I . . . hic . . . I've got . . . hic . . . hiccups . . .
MASTER SW
?
?
?

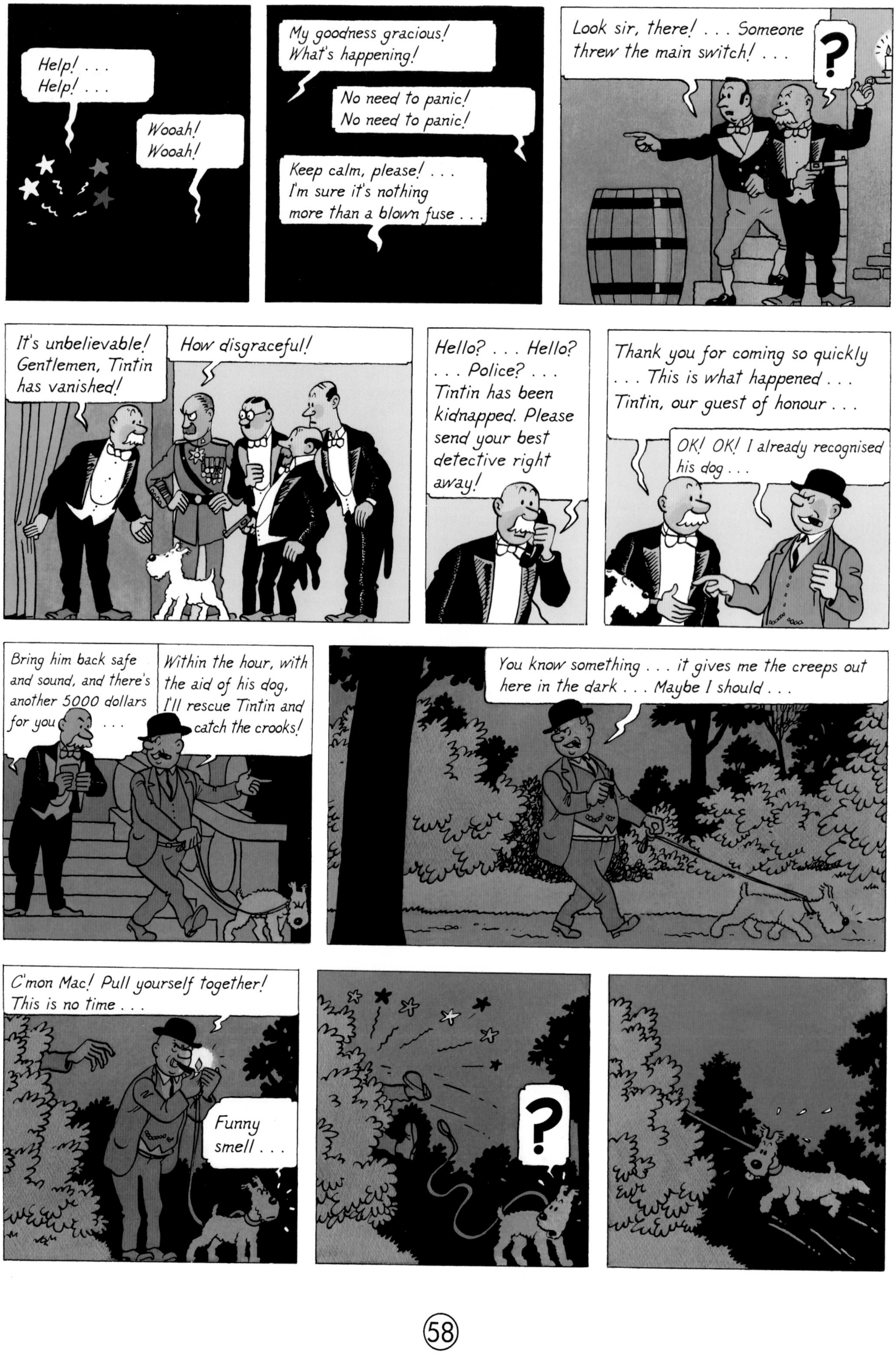
Help! . . .
Help! . . .
Wooah!
Wooah!
My goodness gracious!
What's happening!
No need to panic!
No need to panic!
Keep calm, please! . . .
I'm sure it's nothing
more than a blown fuse . . .
Look sir, there! . . . Someone
threw the main switch! . . .
?
It's unbelievable!
Gentlemen, Tintin
has vanished!
How disgraceful!
Hello? . . . Hello?
. . . Police? . . .
Tintin has been
kidnapped. Please
send your best
detective right
away!
Thank you for coming so quickly
. . . This is what happened . . .
Tintin, our guest of honour . . .
OK! OK! I already recognised
his dog . . .
Bring him back safe
and sound, and there's
another 5000 dollars
for you . . .
Within the hour, with
the aid of his dog,
I'll rescue Tintin and
catch the crooks!
You know something . . . it gives me the creeps out
here in the dark . . . Maybe I should . . .
C'mon Mac! Pull yourself together!
This is no time . . .
Funny
smell . . .
?

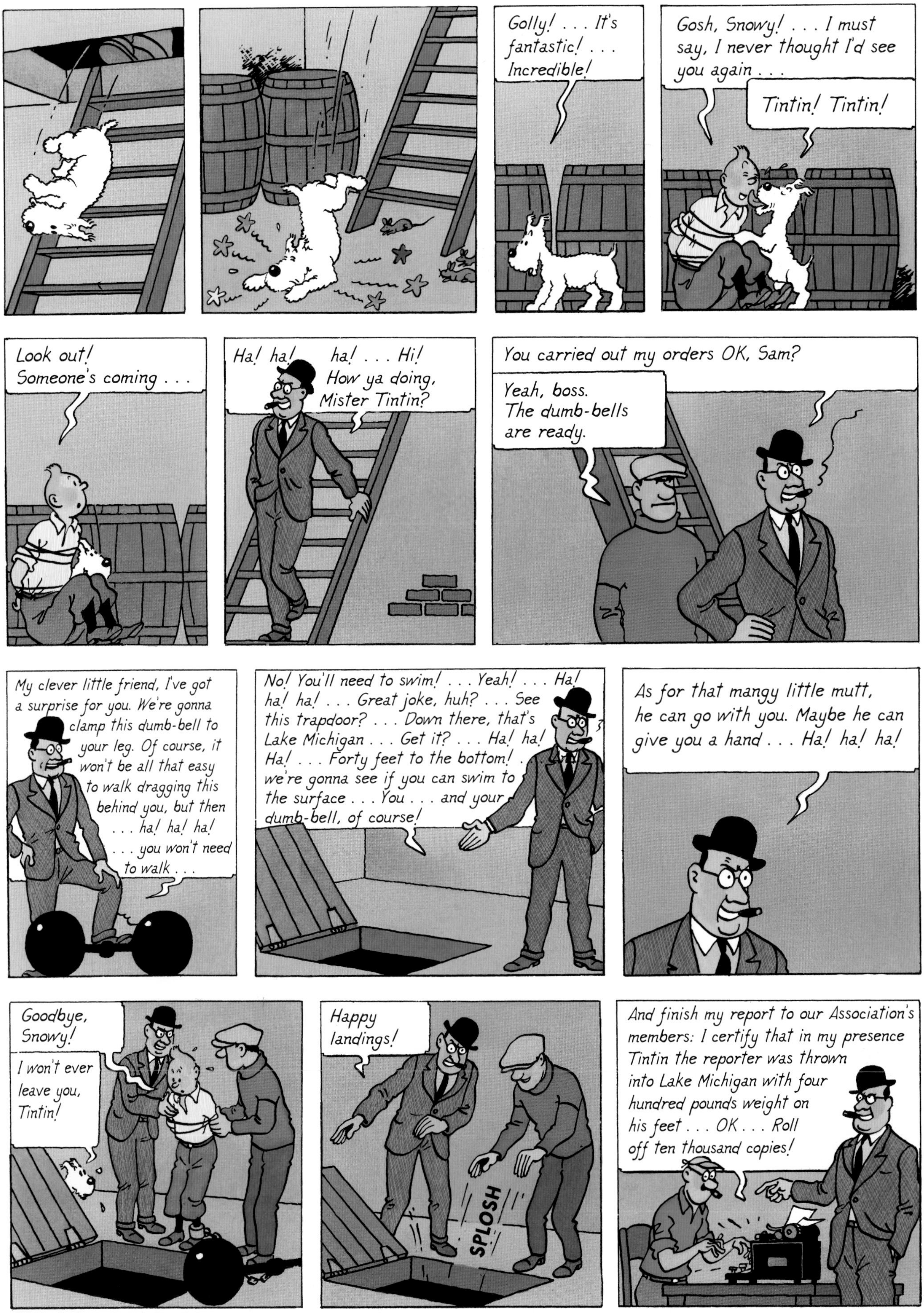

Golly! . . . It's fantastic! . . . Incredible!
Gosh, Snowy! . . . I must say, I never thought I'd see you again . . .
Tintin! Tintin!
Look out! Someone's coming . . .
Ha! ha! ha! . . . Hi! How ya doing, Mister Tintin?
You carried out my orders OK, Sam?
Yeah, boss. The dumb-bells are ready.
My clever little friend, I've got a surprise for you. We're gonna clamp this dumb-bell to your leg. Of course, it won't be all that easy to walk dragging this behind you, but then . . . ha! ha! ha! . . . you won't need to walk . . .
No! You'll need to swim! . . . Yeah! . . . Ha! ha! ha! . . . Great joke, huh? . . . See this trapdoor? . . . Down there, that's Lake Michigan . . . Get it? . . . Ha! ha! Ha! . . . Forty feet to the bottom! . . we're gonna see if you can swim to the surface . . . You . . . and your dumb-bell, of course!
As for that mangy little mutt, he can go with you. Maybe he can give you a hand . . . Ha! ha! ha!
Goodbye, Snowy!
I won't ever leave you, Tintin!
Happy landings!
SPLOSH
And finish my report to our Association's members: I certify that in my presence Tintin the reporter was thrown into Lake Michigan with four hundred pounds weight on his feet . . . OK . . . Roll off ten thousand copies!

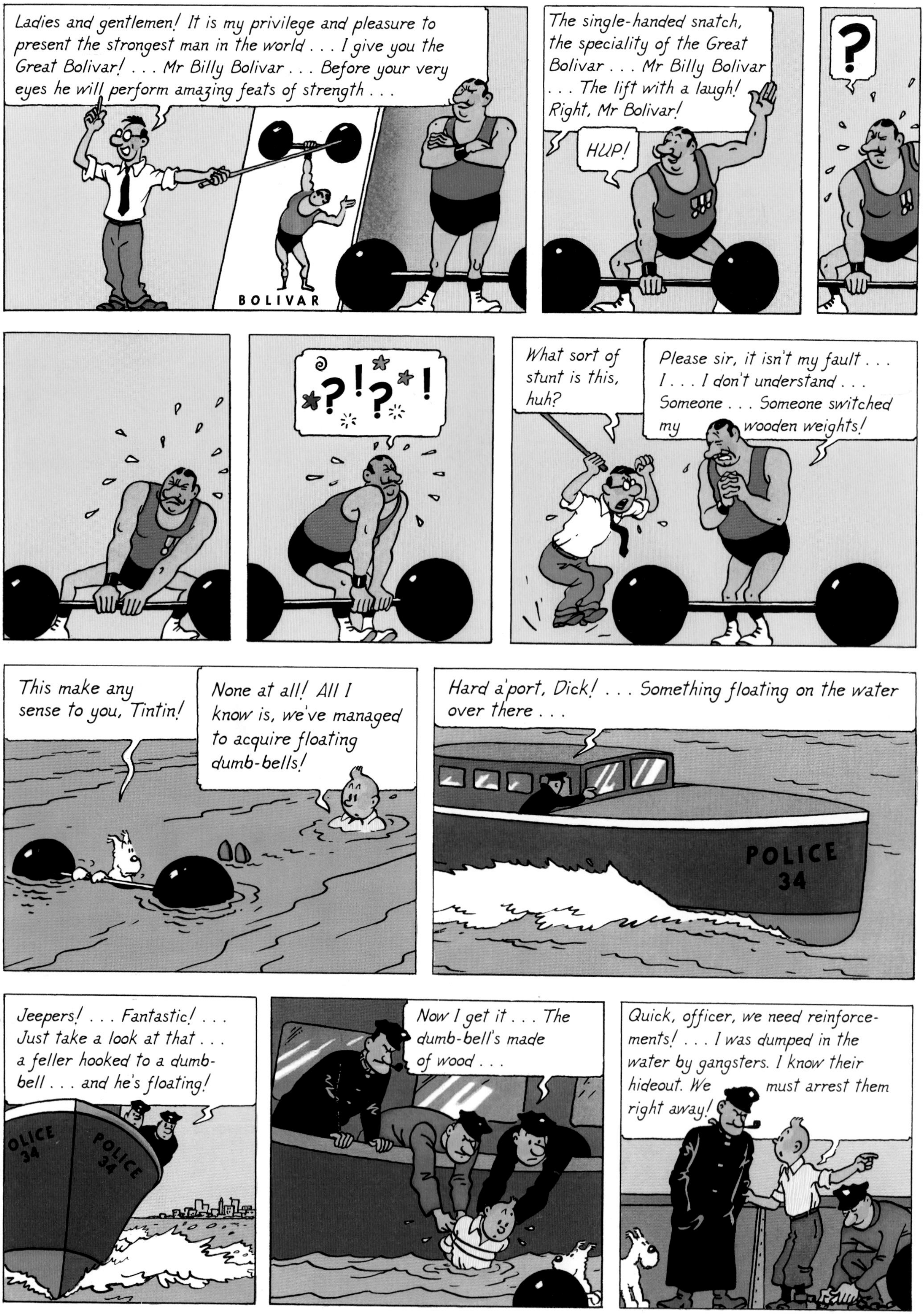

Ladies and gentlemen! It is my privilege and pleasure to present the strongest man in the world . . . I give you the Great Bolivar! . . . Mr Billy Bolivar . . . Before your very eyes he will perform amazing feats of strength . . .
BOLIVAR
The single-handed snatch, the speciality of the Great Bolivar . . . Mr Billy Bolivar . . . The lift with a laugh! Right, Mr Bolivar!
HUP!
?
?!?!
What sort of stunt is this, huh?
Please sir, it isn't my fault . . . I . . . I don't understand . . . Someone . . . Someone switched my wooden weights!
This make any sense to you, Tintin!
None at all! All I know is, we've managed to acquire floating dumb-bells!
Hard a'port, Dick! . . . Something floating on the water over there . . .
POLICE 34
Jeepers! . . . Fantastic! . . . Just take a look at that . . . a feller hooked to a dumb-bell . . . and he's floating!
POLICE 34
Now I get it . . . The dumb-bell's made of wood . . .
Quick, officer, we need reinforcements! . . . I was dumped in the water by gangsters. I know their hideout. We must arrest them right away!

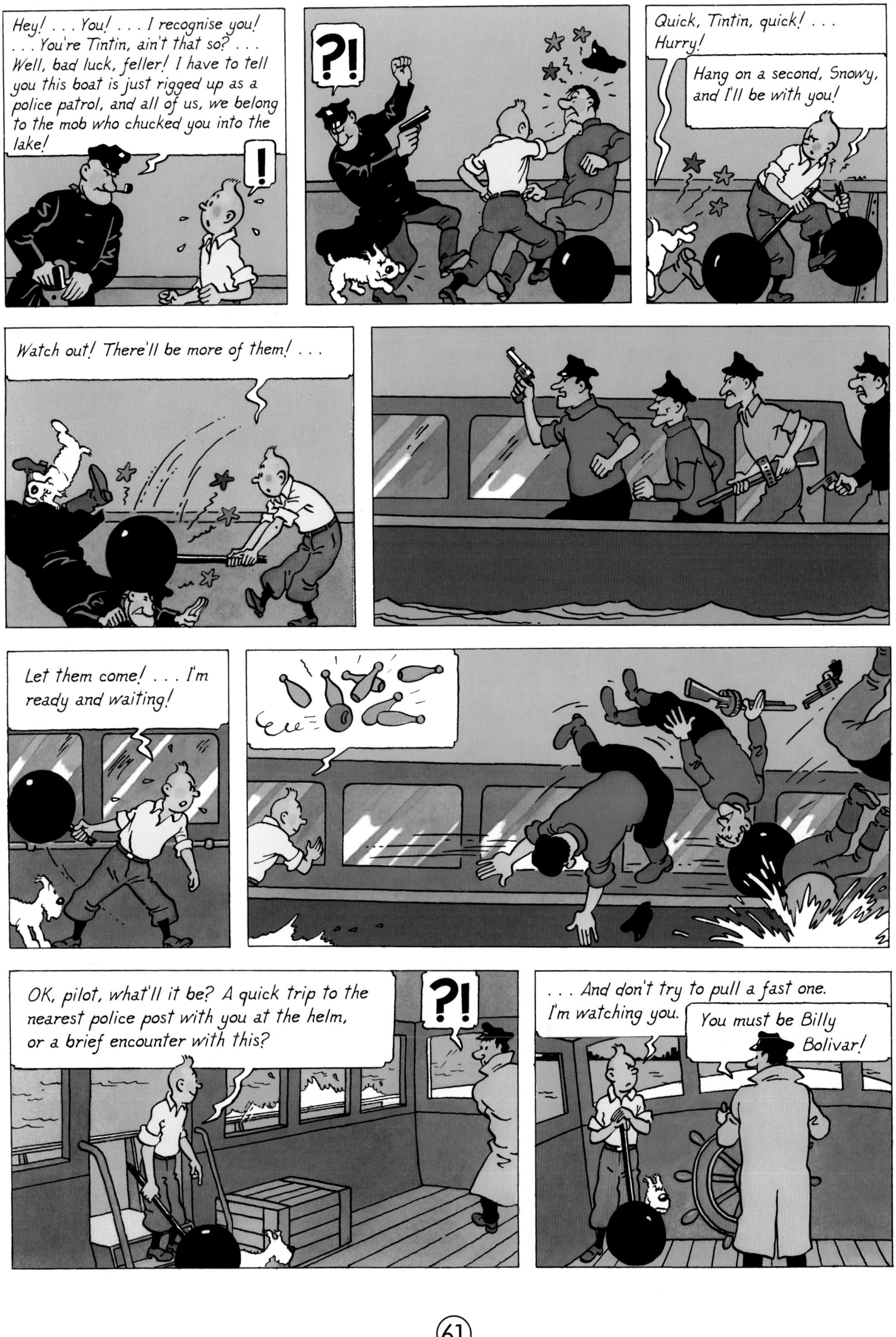

Hey! . . . You! . . . I recognise you! . . . You're Tintin, ain't that so? . . . Well, bad luck, feller! I have to tell you this boat is just rigged up as a police patrol, and all of us, we belong to the mob who chucked you into the lake!
!
?!
Quick, Tintin, quick! . . . Hurry!
Hang on a second, Snowy, and I'll be with you!
Watch out! There'll be more of them! . . .
Let them come! . . . I'm ready and waiting!
OK, pilot, what'll it be? A quick trip to the nearest police post with you at the helm, or a brief encounter with this?
?!
. . . And don't try to pull a fast one. I'm watching you.
You must be Billy Bolivar!

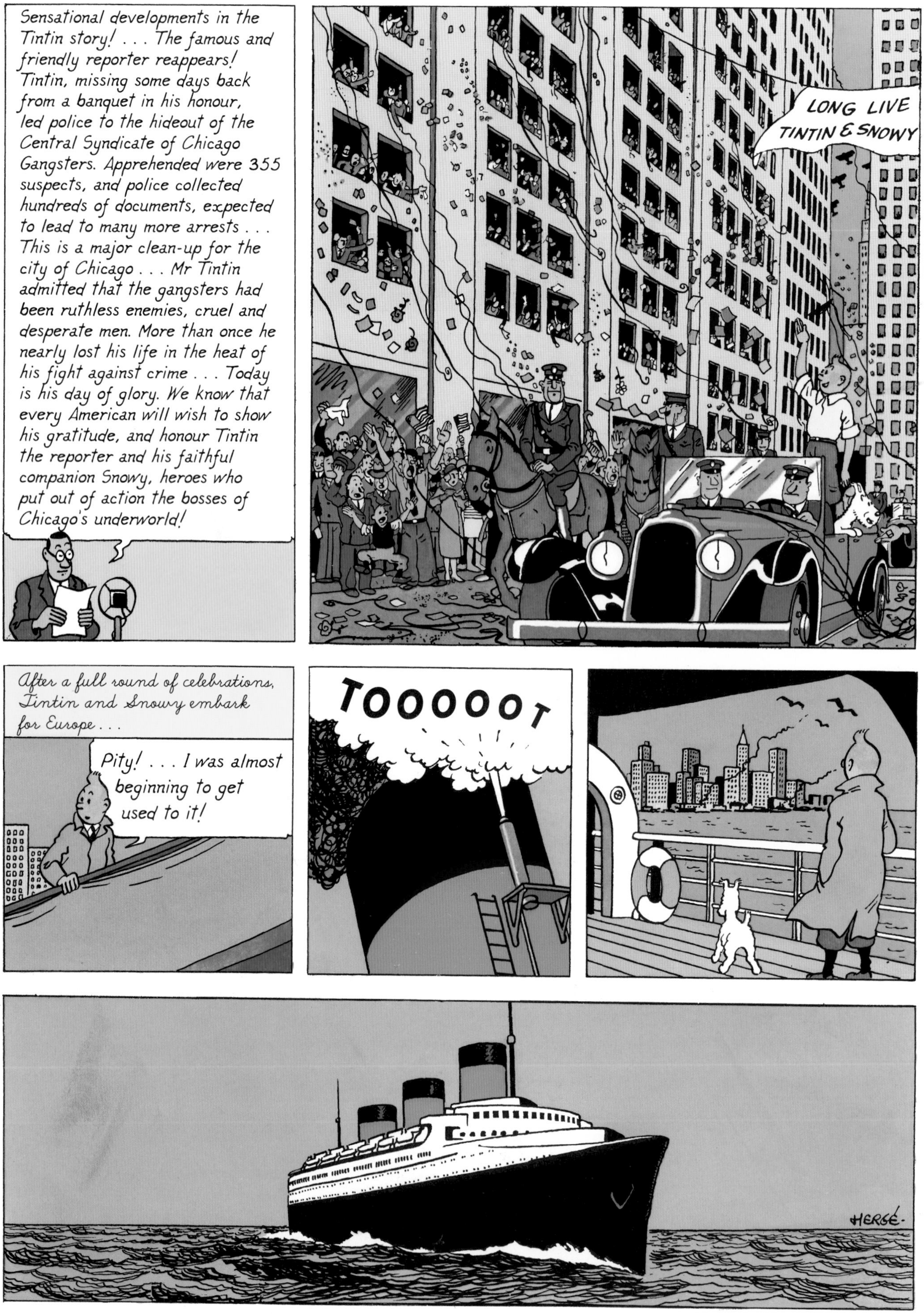
Sensational developments in the Tintin story! . . . The famous and friendly reporter reappears! Tintin, missing some days back from a banquet in his honour, led police to the hideout of the Central Syndicate of Chicago Gangsters. Apprehended were 355 suspects, and police collected hundreds of documents, expected to lead to many more arrests . . . This is a major clean-up for the city of Chicago . . . Mr Tintin admitted that the gangsters had been ruthless enemies, cruel and desperate men. More than once he nearly lost his life in the heat of his fight against crime . . . Today is his day of glory. We know that every American will wish to show his gratitude, and honour Tintin the reporter and his faithful companion Snowy, heroes who put out of action the bosses of Chicago's underworld!
LONG LIVE TINTIN & SNOWY
After a full round of celebrations, Tintin and Snowy embark for Europe . . .
Pity! . . . I was almost beginning to get used to it!
TOOOOOT
HERGÉ